THE DONS OF WARRINGTON

THE DONS OF WARRINGTON TRILOGY BOOK 1

ISOBEL WYCHERLEY

Dedicated to my not-so-twin sister Georgia Wycherley

ACKNOWLEDGMENTS

As always, thank you to my family, friends, and strangers that buy my books. It gets harder to write acknowledgments every time, as I feel like I'm mentioning the same people, but I really couldn't do it without you all- Especially the language translations, provided to me by: Francesco Barone, Jorn Vis, Maximillian Tassev and Merlin Pinkepank.

Even without knowing, you encourage and influence my writing with every interaction we have. There are a lot of new people coming into my life at the moment and I think that's reflected through the mass of interesting characters in this new trilogy.

I hope you enjoy reading this first book, and if you're not begging for the second one, I haven't done my job properly.

Buona Fortuna, mio amico!

PROLOGUE

The SWAT team begin slowly scaling the stairs in formation, their guns swinging from side to side trying to cover all potential vantage points. But it isn't enough. Most of the soldiers are shot dead on the way up, their rigid bodies, covered in heavy armour, slumping down the stairs headfirst like useless, tangled Slinkies.

Sonny reloads using her last ammo clip; she desperately needs to finish them all off with this remaining round of bullets. Within seconds, she guns down over half of the squad with deadly precision. The last two surviving enemies make it to the top of the split staircase, one heading either side towards the girls

They take refuge behind the final pair of columns

on the landing, the only ones to not be riddled with bullet holes.

"How much ammo do you have?" Sonny asks her sister quietly.

"Not a lot," Al replies worriedly.

Sonny exhales heavily. "How long do we have?" she asks, referring to how much time until they're shot by their impending assailants.

Al thinks carefully before she answers, "Five seconds."

Sonny nods defiantly. "Now."

They both quickly drop to their knees and peer around the pillar, their pistols out in front of them. Al squeezes the trigger and the bullet pierces a hole right in between her target's eyes and he slowly slumps to the floor in phases. The legs are the first to go, then the arms, and finally, he falls flat on his face. A crimson river pools out of him and absorbs into the cream carpet, just like syrup trickling into a snow cone.

Sonny pulls the trigger, and the dreaded click of an empty barrel seals her fate. She takes a quick glance from her target to the pistol, and back to look into his eyes. He smirks at her. Her muscles loosen and her blood drains as she comes to terms with death. With a deep breath, she closes her eyes and a deafening shot echoes against the high ceilings.

CHAPTER ONE

Detective Constable Tim Shelley inconspicuously parks his black BMW M5 in a dimly lit, private car park in the centre of Manchester. He opens the driver's side door and places a steady right foot on the tarmac. He makes sure to scour the area first before taking his left foot out of the car, just in case.

He is a man of average height and looks young for his age. His hair is still a dark shade of brown, but is encroached by a few strands of silver bristles at the side of his head. He has a serious face that never seems to break into a smile, unless he's around his loved ones, and he carries with him an air of respect.

He locks the car as he strides towards the small Italian restaurant, Fonty's, on the corner of Princess Street. Its grand-looking, cream marble staircase invites you in with its whispers of elegance. As he approaches, the front doors swing open and the smell of freshly baked garlic bread spills out onto the streets outside. He takes a deep breath; his mouth begins to water.

"Hello, Mr Shelley," announces a tall, gentle-looking man who has dark features, but completely lacks hair on his head and face and probably on the rest of his body, too, thinks Tim. "If you'd like to come with me, I'll show you to your table." He holds out his arm and smiles, welcoming Shelley in.

Shelley trails behind the man, taking notice of the hordes of customers who are chatting rapidly, and eating even quicker. There's something about Italian restaurants that make them louder than any other cuisine, Shelley thinks to himself.

They reach an empty, red velvet booth and the waiter beckons Shelley to sit. He takes another look around the restaurant before stiffly sitting down on the soft-cushioned bench.

The man smiles. "Can I get you a drink, a menu?"

"I'll have a water... and maybe some of that garlic bread, please," Shelley requests, unable to resist his temptations and hunger.

The man smiles more brightly now. "Excellent

choice, sir. Our garlic bread is the best in the city." With that, he spins around to fetch Shelley's order.

Shelley can't help but feel on edge. The meeting was set up in a friendly manner, but there's always the possibility that the Mafia are just coaxing him into their territory to get rid of him quietly and without witnesses. Thankfully, he decided to bring his gun with him tonight.

The waiter returns with a glass of water and a plate of garlic bread. He carefully places them onto the table, then leans in closer to Shelley.

"My name is Calvino. My father, Don Fontana, will be with you shortly." He says this without expression, straightens up, and continues to serve other customers.

Shelley begins to shift in his seat now, but is comforted by the fact that the meeting will take place in the midst of a bustling restaurant. He takes a gulp of cold water and picks at the edges of his garlic bread. It's as delectable as he had imagined.

As Shelley is demolishing his first slice of garlic bread, the staff door swings open casually, and a short, broad-shouldered old man emerges, wearing a stylish pinstripe suit. For a man of his age, he has a thick head of salt and pepper hair, combed into a stylish sweep across his forehead. He has a little curly moustache, like Poirot, that makes his face look even more handsome. It is clear to Shelley that this is The Don. There is a shield of intimidation surrounding the man. The waiting staff rush to look busy and avoid even glancing in his direction.

"Mr Shelley, how wonderful to see you!" He extends his hand for Shelley to shake.

Tim stands up to greet him, taking his hand firmly. "Mr Fontana," he says bluntly, making sure to hold defiant eye contact.

"What do you think of the garlic bread, it's delicious, no?" The handsome old man smiles as he sits down on the opposite side of the booth.

"Yes, it's very nice."

"Do you mind if I have a piece myself?" Don Fontana asks, with raised eyebrows.

"Go for it." Shelley waves dismissively, grabbing a slice for himself as well.

Don Fontana takes a hefty bite out of the bread. "Mmm, *fantastico*." He kisses his fingers. "So... Mr. Shelley, you wanted to talk with me about something."

"Yes. It's about the Baulsack family," Shelley explains.

Don Fontana licks the melted cheese off of his thumb and throws his arms up in disgust. "Ugh! Those barbarians. I condemn the day they arrived in this city, bringing with them their vile behaviour and unsolicited violence. Did you know they killed my cousin's son? He was no trouble to them; he had just started university."

"I'm aware of that, yes. How come you didn't retaliate?" Shelley quizzes.

"We are not usually violent, Detective. My cousin just wanted to move on with his life, and his remaining family, they went back to Italy. Those Germans on the other hand, they love violence."

"I know. I'm trying to eradicate them from the country, but, as you probably know, the other detectives are receiving bribes from the family and won't help me. That's why I've come to you."

Don Fontana's eyes light up and he leans a little closer to Shelley over the table. "You want my help?" He smiles.

"Yes. Nothing much, I just need you to tell me where I can find Helmut Baulsack. It's a win-win for us both. I get to do my job and keep people safe and you get to put your family's killer behind bars."

Don Fontana lets out a little laugh, raspy from chain-smoking. "You won't find Helmut here. He is still operating in Germany. The man you're looking for is his brother, Holdis."

"Holdis Baulsack... Is that a real name?" Shelley asks.

"None of them sound like real names, they're ridiculous!" Don Fontana lets out a hearty laugh.

Shelley smirks slightly, too. "So where can I find him?"

"I will write down an address. That is where he

7

lives, you should find him there. Excuse me while I retrieve the information for you." He stands up from the table in a slow and intimidating manner, nods gently to Shelley and strolls back through the staff door.

Shelley continues to eat the rest of the now slightly cold garlic bread on the plate as he looks around at the customers. He wishes he could bring his own family here for dinner one night, but that's too dangerous.

Don Fontana reappears, this time holding a small piece of paper in his hand. Shelley rises from his chair, ready to leave after receiving the tiny scrap of hope.

"Here you are, my friend." They shake hands and Don Fontana deposits the note into Shelley's hand.

"Thank you, Mr Fontana."

"Please, call me Don." He smiles. "We're friends now."

He nods. "Pleasure doing business with you, Don."

"You're home late," Karen says to her husband.

"I was just finishing up on a lead. I think I've got them."

"The Germans?" She spins around from the sink to look at him.

He lets out a small sigh. "Well, not all of them, but it's a start."

"That's great. Well done, honey." She smiles and kisses him on the cheek. "You smell of garlic. Have you had your tea?"

"Erm, yeah. I got something from the canteen at work, thank you, darling." He kisses her cheek this time.

"The girls are outside." She smiles at him and wanders back into the kitchen.

Shelley walks out of the back door and spots his daughters smoking and chatting on the swing bench. He doesn't like them smoking, but even Shelley himself cannot fight the urge.

"Hey, girls. How are you both?" he asks, sitting on the small wicker stool next to the garden table.

"Good, thanks!" they both chirp,

"How are you?" Sonya asks him.

"Yeah, I'm alright." He sighs. "Could do with one of those, though." He points to their cigarettes.

Alice slides the pack across the table to him. He puts one in his mouth and looks cross-eyed at the end while he lights it, breathing it in as it burns.

"What did you do at work today?" Alice quizzes.

"Nothing new really, you know I'm not supposed to discuss it with you. I made a lot of progress on it today, though."

"Well, that's good then. One step closer to having

your very own Baulsack!" Sonya jokes and they all laugh.

"You know he's got a brother, Holdis?" Shelley tells them, waiting for them to pick up on the funny side.

"Holdis Baulsack?" The girls burst into laughter. "That can't be a real name!"

"That's what I said!" Shelley joins in.

"His parents mustn't have liked him," Alice reckons.

"At least they didn't call him Sonya." Sonya rolls her eyes; she's always hated her own name.

"What – Sonya Baulsack? Ha-ha," Alice teases.

"You've got a lovely name!" Shelley tries not to laugh. "What's wrong with Sonya?"

Her face is deadpan. "Everything."

Alice nods. "She's got a point. Right, I'm off to bed." She pushes herself up from the bench.

"Me too." Sonya joins her.

They both give their father a hug and a kiss before re-entering the house. They carry out the same ritual with their mother, and head upstairs to bed.

CHAPTER TWO

Early the next morning, Tim Shelley prepares to ambush Holdis Baulsack at his Manchester residence. He sits at his desk in his cosy office, contemplating his plan of action. Every scheme he's conjured up so far has resulted in him being dead when he simulates it in his mind.

How the hell am I going to do this alone? he thinks to himself. He cups his head in his palms, trying to think of a new plan. He has to get it done today.

"Alright, Dad?" Alice asks through the crack in the door.

He jolts in momentary surprise and swizzles around on his chair to face her. "Yeah, I'm alright, darling. I just can't think of a way to catch Holdis without getting myself killed," he admits reluctantly.

Alice walks over to his desk and rests her hand on his shoulder. She looks at the desk and observes the blueprints of Holdis's residence.

"Wait, is that in Deansgate?" Alice asks.

"Yeah."

"I've been there before! Dad, I know how you can get in." She smiles excitedly and rocks him back and forth by his shoulders. All that truanting from her first year of college is finally starting to pay off.

"How?" he asks hesitantly. He doesn't want to get her involved, but he'll take all the help he can get.

"This balcony here." She points to it on the paper. "If you look at the apartment blocks next door..." she explains as she pulls up maps on the computer, "you could easily jump from there onto the balcony, then through a window, or the door if you want to be boring about it." She nudges him.

Shelley checks the plan over, simulating it in his head again. "That won't work, he has guards there with him all day." He shakes his head glumly.

"I can distract them for you. They're not going to be suspicious of me, are they?"

He shakes his head more viciously now. "No. I'm not putting you in danger."

"What've you been training us for then, nothing?"

"Your own protection!" he shouts.

"What's going on?" Sonya appears in the doorway now.

They stop their arguing to look at her.

"Nothing," Shelley quips.

"Dad won't let me help him pull off the only plan that'll work," Alice counteracts.

"What plan?"

Alice explains it to her briefly and all the while Shelley sits back, listening, impressed with her planning but still not willing to let them help.

Sonya's eyes light up. "I'll help, too."

"No! Neither of you are getting involved in this," Shelley insists.

"Come on, Dad. You know we can do it! Plus, we've got nothing to do now college is over."

"And how am I supposed to get him into my police car, hey? Walk him right past his guards, straight through his front door?" Shelley procrastinates.

"No, Dad, don't be stupid... Out the *back* door. His guards won't be there because we're going to lure them outside. Jeez, don't you know I'm better than that?" Alice rolls her eyes.

"Come on, it's worth a shot, innit?" Sonya urges him to agree.

He thinks about it for a very long time before answering, "Let's give it a go then, girls. Don't tell your mother I've let you do this, or anyone for that matter. She'll have a heart attack." He wipes his damp forehead with the back of his hand.

The girls shout in excitement and hug each other

like they're footballers who've just won the league, pushing and shoving each other around playfully.

———

Shelley has never been so nervous as he pulls into the multi-storey car park, not far from the apartment blocks and the building that Holdis bought and had renovated into his personal home. Sonya is in the passenger seat, Alice in the back.

"Right. Let's go over the plan," Shelley orders.

"Okay, so, Dad, you need to get to the roof of the apartment building. I've done that before, you literally just need to take the lift to the fifth floor, go through the double doors and then up the stairwell to the top," Alice explains.

"Why've you been on the roof before?" Shelley frowns.

"Dad, please, I'll take questions at the end," she diverts tactically. "Me and Sonny will make our way to his house and lure the bodyguards out into the street. You can then bring Holdis round the back, out of sight. Then we'll finish up and drive this car back home."

"Sounds good." Shelley nods.

"Is your patrol car in place?" Sonya asks.

"Yeah. Everything's ready," Shelley confirms.

"Let's go then." Alice pats them both on the shoulder from the back seat.

Before they part, Shelley gives his daughters a long-drawn-out hug and kisses them on the forehead.

"Please be safe," he tells them.

They both roll their eyes. "Yeah, yeah. Come on, let's go."

Shelley paces to the apartment building and waits for the lift to appear on the ground floor. The girls, trailing behind slightly, wait until they see the doors meet and their dad disappear behind the metal curtains before they make their way to Holdis Baulsack's front door.

"Ready?" Sonya asks her twin sister.

"Ready, lad," she replies, before running a few paces down the road and collapsing on the ground.

Sonya takes a deep breath and thinks upsetting thoughts like dead puppies and losing yet another game of chess. Her eyes begin to swell with tears. She's ready. She frantically knocks on the door and begins to shout for help.

"Please help me! My sister has just collapsed! Please help!"

Two guards appear at the door with angry expressions on their faces – that is, until they spot a young, baby-faced girl with tears streaming down her face. Her short, mousy brown hair flicks carelessly over her forehead and she's wearing an all-black outfit, apart from the colourful overshirt that dances around her in the breeze.

"Vhat's going on?" The German guard's expression softens and he looks slightly worried.

"I'm not sure, she just collapsed. I'm not sure if she's breathing," Sonya explains.

She points to her sister, a little heap on the ground. Her blonde plaits are sprawled above her head like devil horns – an unplanned allusion that will surely be missed by the guards. She isn't hard to spot in bright red tartan dungarees, with metal chains that glimmer in the sunlight.

The guards rush out of the house and over to her, leaving the front door open behind them. Sonya takes a quick peep inside but sees nobody. They crouch down next to Alice and turn her onto her back. Alice tries her hardest not to breathe too heavily so that they can't see her chest rising and falling. Sonya joins them and tries to distract them for as long as possible.

"She's still got a pulse," one guard proclaims, his sausage-like finger pressed against Alice's neck.

Sonya lets out a puff of air. "Thank God!"

"Vhat's her name?"

"Sandy."

Sonya clocks Alice's eyebrow twitch slightly. She knows she hates that name.

"Zandy, can you hear me?" the other guard asks the unresponsive stranger on the floor.

No response.

"Try singing to her, she likes that."

The guards frown. "Vhy don't *you* zing to her?"

"Vocal injury." She pouts, holding her throat, making her voice croaky now.

The guards look at each other for a moment, both trying to urge the other to sing,

"I know an old German lullaby..." one of them says sheepishly.

"Oh, yeah, do that!" Sonya beams.

He leans in closer to her, clears his throat, and in a hushed warble begins to sing,

"*Weißt du, wie viel Sternlein stehen...*" (Do you know how many stars there are...)

Meanwhile, Shelley has made it to the roof. He looks down at the drop to the balcony. It doesn't seem too far. He braces himself and jumps off the edge. He lands with a crash and rolls forward towards the door. It is quiet for a while as Shelley regains his bearings, but not for long.

Thud. Thud. Thud.

The ominous noise gains speed, the closer to Shelley it gets. Startled, he straightens himself up and pulls out his gun.

Holdis, a fat, red-faced man, strides through the balcony doors, his chins wobbling violently with even the slightest bit of movement,

"Who ze hell are you? *Guaaaaaards!*" he bellows. His voice is so deep and broad, you can almost feel yourself falling endlessly through his giant lungs.

"I'm Detective Tim Shelley, you're under arrest!"

Holdis looks around for his guards, but once he realises they are nowhere to be seen, he scowls and holds his hands up in surrender. He begins rambling angrily in German and Shelley makes no attempt to decipher what he's saying. His daughters would know, though, he thinks momentarily, but that just makes him panic about what is going on downstairs and so he snaps back into detective mode.

Shelley quickly cuffs Holdis and forces him down the couple of flights of stairs to the ground floor, though he doesn't go easily. Sonya takes another look towards the house and spots her dad carting Holdis through the bottom floor of the building. Holdis clocks that the door is open and begins shouting in German, in order to get his guards' attention,

"*Dass sie nun so fröhlich sind...*" (And they're all so happy now...)

"Ahhhhhh!" Sonya interrupts the song to cover up Holdis's pleas. "Our dad is going to be so worried!" Sonya says, turning to her sister again and taking hold of her hand.

Alice begins to rouse and she blinks rapidly, looking around as if she hadn't really been here this whole time.

"*Mein Gott*, I sink ze singing vorked!"

"What happened?" Alice frowns.

"You're okay. Let's get you home." Sonya picks

her sister up off the floor with the help of one of the guards.

The higher they lift her, the more weight she puts on their hands, so that they keep dropping her to the floor, her limbs loosely flapping around. Sonya tries not to laugh, knowing what she's doing. Finally, they drag her to her feet. They say thank-you to the guards before stumbling off down the road.

Once the guards are back inside the house, they break into a sprint back to their dad's car in the multi-storey.

"What was all that about? You looked like Gillian McKeith." Sonya laughs.

"I was just making it a bit light-hearted."

Sonya shakes her head in disbelief. "You could've got us killed!"

"Didn't though, did I?" She raises her eyebrows, "And, also, Sandy?" She pulls a face. "Come on."

They drive home and await a phone call from their dad. It arrives a couple of hours later.

"We got him. Thanks for your help, girls, I shouldn't have doubted you," Shelley booms through the loudspeaker.

"No probs, Dad. It was a fun day out," they say respectively.

"Well, don't get used to it, it was a one-time thing," Shelley orders.

The girls look at each other in disappointment. "Alright," they chorus.

"I'll see you tonight, love you," he tells them.

"See ya," they reply, before hanging up.

"I wish he'd let us get more involved, that was fun," Alice says to her sister.

Sonya nods in agreement. "I know. We need something that lets us use all these mad skills he's been teaching us our whole lives. Otherwise, what's the point?"

"Maybe one day," Alice hopes.

"Maybe one day I'll have a six-foot penis, but it's never gonna happen, is it?"

CHAPTER THREE

Detective Shelley does not receive a hero's welcome when he arrives at the police station herding a giant, angry German, as he's just captured the man that bulks up their pay cheques. But Shelley has him now, and there is nothing they can do about it publicly. Hordes of reporters are waiting outside, desperate to capture a picture of the man the country has been in fear of for years.

Shelley gets a stern talking-to from his peers about how he didn't act on official police business to make the arrest, and they force him to be the one that addresses the mob that's forming outside.

"I will. A great justice was done today," he says defiantly.

"Why can't you just take bribes like the rest of us? I can't afford to take my family on holiday this year now, thanks to you!" one of the detectives whines.

"Maybe you're in the wrong profession then." Shelley stands his ground.

He walks out of the main doors to address the media.

"Hello, everybody. At one-fifteen pm today, an arrest was made on... Holdis Baulsack." A few chuckles arise from the crowd. He ignores them and continues.

"Holdis is the brother of the German Mafia's leader, Helmut. With this arrest, we have weakened the Mafia family's power within the Manchester district, and, hopefully, going forward, we can make more arrests to completely eradicate this disease that has plagued our country in recent years." He concludes, "That is all, thank you."

He retreats back into the station, allowing reporters to scream questions at the back of his head as he leaves.

The live news reports do not go unnoticed by Don Marco Fontana, who is sitting in his home office, sipping cognac and smoking cigarettes with his son and *consigliere*, Mario Fontana.

A call comes through on the landline. The Don's secretary informs him it is Detective Leaver calling from the Metropolitan Police. She puts him through,

"Yes?" Don Fontana answers bluntly, a cigarette hanging loosely out of his mouth.

"Marco. I want you to know that everybody in the force knows it was you who gave Shelley that address. If one Mafia family is going down, then you all are. We're coming for you, you fucking greaseballs." The phoneline drops and the high-pitched ringing buzzes through Don Fontana's ears.

His face never changes. He gently places the phone back on the receiver, takes a drag on his cigarette and turns to his son. "Get Shelley on the phone, set up a meeting for tonight," he orders Mario.

"Of course, Don. Where?" Mario asks.

"The restaurant is fine," he says and waves his son out of the room.

Shelley rushes towards the restaurant, hoping he'd never have to come here again. The charm only worked the first time. As Calvino opens the door to greet him, he walks straight past him with no more than a quick nod. This time, however, the restaurant is empty and scarcely lit. Shelley panics and turns to head back for the door, but Calvino blocks his path.

"Don't worry. Don Fontana will be here any second," he mutters.

Right on cue, he appears. "Detective Shelley! Come, sit." The Don beckons to the seat in front of the one he's just perched on. "Come, it won't take long," he urges a reluctant Shelley again.

Shelley cautiously strolls over and sits on the small, elegant chair and declines any food or drink this time. "What's this about?" he asks.

"Remember that little favour I did for you?"

"Of course."

"Well, now it's your turn to repay me."

"No. You didn't say anything about returning the favour." Shelley shakes his head.

"Oh, but I did. I told you that you are my friend. Friends help each other out, no?" He frowns.

Shelley doesn't reply, he just stares at the floor shaking his head, thinking that he should have seen this coming.

The Don tries to persuade him. "It's only a *little* favour."

Shelley finally replies, "What is it?"

"Kill Detective Leaver."

"What? You don't actually expect me to do that, do you?"

Don Fontana nods. "I help you, you help me."

"No. I can't do that. I won't kill another human being, let alone one of my colleagues."

The Don thinks this answer over and slowly nods again. "Okay, Mr Shelley. But on your head be it."

"So, you're threatening me now?"

"I will do what I have to do."

They stare each other down across the table for what seems like forever, before Don Fontana breaks the tense silence. "You can go now," he says, staying in his seat.

They watch each other for a moment longer before Shelley uses the table to push himself out of his chair, looking around for any Italians lurking in the darkness, ready to pounce on him. But there aren't any. He leaves without another word from anyone and makes his way back to his car.

On the drive home, he is constantly looking in his rear-view mirror for anyone that might be following him. He makes it back unscathed and hugs his family tight, to their confusion. He calls his daughters into his office to talk in private, out of earshot of their mother.

"I'm in a lot of trouble over this, girls, at work and with the Mafia families. I want you to promise me that you'll stay safe and stick together. Come to me if you come across any trouble from anyone," he orders them.

"Alright, Dad," they say, unconcerned.

They exit the study and grin at each other. They think he is overreacting and being too protective of them, or maybe he just doesn't trust them enough. But they know their own capabilities, and soon, the Fontanas will, too.

CHAPTER FOUR

A fter a couple of weeks of following the girls, they have a good enough understanding of what their schedule is, and finally decide to ambush them as they leave their regular Wednesday activity – shooting. It's a new hobby of theirs, Sonya's especially, since it requires very minimal movement.

She sits steadily on the chair; the bolt action rifle is pushed firmly against her shoulder. She takes a long, deep breath in, her eyes focus on the target. She slowly releases the air through her nose and, once her body reaches the peak of its stillness, she unleashes a storm of golden slugs, one after another, reloading in the blink of an eye.

Ten rounds of bullets pierce a perfect hole in the centre of the bullseye before she even needs to take a breath in.

"I can do better than that," Alice jokes.

"I'd like to see you try."

Alice places the gun on her shoulder, lines the sight up with the bullseye and steadies her breathing. At peak stillness, she pulls the trigger. The gap between reloads is longer than Sonya's and there are ten bullet holes speckled in the bullseye.

"Well, it did the job, that's all I can say." Alice shrugs.

"Unless I was there, then they'd already be dead by the time you'd shot one bullet."

Alice raises her eyebrow at this. "Ooh, you're hard!"

They both emerge from the entrance of the shooting range, chatting and laughing with each other. They are standing outside the car having a cigarette when they are grabbed from behind, handcuffed and blindfolded in a matter of seconds. They put up a struggle, but strong hands grip their arms tightly against their bodies, so that any movement is impossible.

They are loaded into a car; by the sound of the doors closing, Alice reckons it's an Alfa Romeo. As they're driven to their unknown destination, she also memorises the directions in which the car is turning. Whilst Alice is doing this, Sonya manages to free herself from the handcuffs, and discreetly begins unlocking Alice's as well. They wait patiently for the car to come to a stop.

The brakes squeal, and the handbrake is applied. The two men in the front seats get out of the car to begin to escort the girls into the family restaurant. They open the doors simultaneously as they both scout out the area, checking for police or other enemies.

"Nice Alfa." Alice smiles, blindfold still intact.

Sonya, also blindfolded, throws her cuffs out of the door, onto the floor of the car park and removes her own blindfold. "Bet you can't guess what colour it is," she says to her sister. All the while, the Italians look on in astonishment.

Alice ponders the question for a moment. "I'm gonna go with... black," she says, taking her blindfold off after her guess.

She leans her head out of the door and sees the black paintwork reflecting the street lights. "Get in!" She fist-bumps the air.

"That was such a fluke!" Sonya laughs.

They get out of the car and shut the doors behind them.

"So, where are we? Considering the journey lasted fifteen minutes, travelling primarily south, I would say we were in Manchester... or somewhere round there." Alice smiles at the tall, muscly Italian man towering over her.

"W-we're in Manchester," Mario stutters.

"Is that an Italian restaurant?" Sonya asks, pointing to the building, excited at the thought of some good food.

"Erm... yes," Mario replies.

"Look, if you wanted to take us out on a double date, kidnapping us wasn't the way to go about it. We never turn down Italian food, though, do we, Sonny?"

"We definitely do not," Sonny replies, beginning to strut towards the back entrance of the building.

Mario follows behind them, confused and astonished by how calm they are after being kidnapped and taken hostage. The driver gets back into his Alfa, making his way back to the Fontanas' gated community.

Mario takes them to a red velvet booth in the empty eatery and tells them to wait there while he gathers the rest of his family who are in the restaurant. Three well-dressed men and a beautiful, stylish woman appear, standing in front of the table, sizing up the girls with no subtlety whatsoever.

The first man is Mario Fontana. Tall, well-built and handsome, he has thick, pitch-black hair scraped back onto his head, minus the tiny curl of hair that sits perfectly on his olive-coloured forehead. He has a small scar across his right eyebrow that fits in well with the darkness that seems to surround his smouldering hazel eyes.

The second is Mario's youngest brother, Luca.

He is much smaller than the other two men and he wears a pair of stylish round spectacles that bring out the greenness of his eyes. He has a head of jet-black curly hair, almost to perm standards. His body language is also a lot more cautious and he gives off the vibe that he is not a very confident man.

The final man is Calvino Fontana, The Don's least favourite son, though he won't admit it. Not only does he want nothing to do with the illegal dealings of his family, but he also looks completely different to his entire family, having no hair whatsoever, not even eyebrows. But he doesn't look old at all, more like Mark Strong. There isn't a single wrinkle or crease on his face, he's like a pristine, shiny egg on legs.

The woman, an absolute beauty, is Bella Fontana. Out of her and her sister, she is her father's favourite daughter. She has thick, long, black hair, lightly curled so that it falls gently onto her shoulders. Her plump lips are painted scarlet, but the rest of her soft-featured face is makeup free, she doesn't need it. She uses her beauty to persuade officials to look the other way whenever the Fontanas get caught out in something illegal. She hasn't failed to change their minds yet!

"Who are you lovely bunch of people?" Sonya asks, smiling.

"We're the Fontana family. This is our restaurant," Calvino explains.

"Brilliant! Can we get a coupla menus, please?" Alice asks.

Calvino looks at Mario and he shrugs to signal *why not*. He walks over to the reception desk and picks up a couple of menus and hands them to the girls.

They run their fingers down the menu and tap their chins comically to seem as though they're thinking their order over.

"I'll have one of everything, thanks," Sonya orders.

"I'll have the same, cheers," Alice adds, holding her menu out to Calvino.

"Everything? I don't know if I can do that."

"Customer's always right," Sonya quips.

Calvino takes the menus and plasters a fake smile on his face. "Okay, I'll see what I can do." He scuttles off into the kitchen, leaving the girls with Mario, Luca and Bella.

Nobody says anything for a long time. The background noise of Calvino bashing pots and pans around seems to be amplified in the empty restaurant. Alice looks around the room, noting the empty tables.

"Get a lot of customers then?" she asks, with a smirk that's mimicked by Sonya.

"We're closed," Mario replies.

"Ah. So, we're a private party, are we? Don't remember booking this in."

"You're here as hostages, you idiots!" Bella butts in out of frustration.

Alice frowns. "Hostages for what?"

"Your father owes us a favour and he won't do it for us. So, now we just wait until he notices you haven't come home. He'll know where to find you," Mario explains calmly.

"You know our dad, how?" Sonya asks.

"We're on the same football team," Mario says sarcastically.

"Are you! Have you seen his right footers? Absolute shambles." The girls laugh.

Mario frowns. "I was joking... Haven't you heard of our family?"

The girls look at each other and shrug. "Nope."

Calvino emerges with a plate of garlic bread and a bowl of meatballs. He places them onto the table, saying, "Your lasagne and risotto are still cooking."

The girls dig in before the plate even touches the table. They haven't eaten in two hours, that's practically enough time to starve to death.

"We're an Italian Mafia family. The Fontanas... I can't believe you've never heard of us," Mario says, his pride hurt a little.

"What's our dad got to do with you lot?" Sonya asks, with a mouthful of garlic bread.

"He came to us, to help him find Holdis Baulsack," Mario explains.

The girls begin silently giggling with their

mouths full of food. "MeatBaulsacks," Alice mumbles, pointing to the bowl of meatballs, making Sonya laugh even harder.

"What is with these two?" Bella whispers to her brothers, before walking back into the staff area, unamused.

Mario smirks; he quite likes their childish nature, something he and his siblings had had to grow out of very quickly. He takes a seat in the booth with them.

"So, what do you want from Dad, then?" Alice asks him.

"I can't tell you."

"Go on. We came up with the plan to help him capture lil ol' Baulsack," she urges.

He thinks about it for a moment, looking at Luca for advice as he's always been the smart, sensible one.

"We need him to kill a detective that's been giving us a hard time," Luca explains.

"We can do it," Alice offers, ripping the garlic bread with her teeth like a proud animal that's just tucking into its freshly captured prey.

Mario laughs. "I don't think you could."

"Are you joking? You can't say you weren't impressed by what we did before," Sonya says, her thumb pointing backwards in time. "We know exactly what we're doing."

Mario knows this is true. He ponders it, looking at Luca again, who also seems to be genuinely considering it.

"Here's something that ought to be the clincher of deals," Alice begins to tell the brothers. "There's a man outside, one of Holdis's guards. He's been circling the building for five and a half minutes or thereabouts. It takes him twenty-five point four-six seconds to do a complete lap around the building. And I know exactly how to get him."

The brothers look at each other, and then to the windows. There is nobody outside, apart from a couple, arm in arm, gazing into each other's eyes like there's nothing else going on in the world.

Luca turns back to Alice. "There's nobody there."

"Not yet, be discreet about it," she orders, and they all begin to side-eye the window on the far side of the building.

"Ten... nine... three-two-one." As soon as she says *one*, a man, dressed in all black, wanders past the window, looking in.

Sonya recognises him, too, from the day they helped their dad to capture Holdis. Maybe the Germans had been following them, too, but the Fontanas had just gotten there first.

"What's your plan then?" Luca asks out of curiosity and the desire to be out of danger.

"You can watch it in action." Alice smiles, then turns to her sister. "Did you see the ladder at the back of the building?"

"No," Sonya admits. She never takes notice of anything.

Alice rolls her eyes, "Course you didn't. Anyway, all you need to do is wait for him to be below you, drop down on him, then do 'the thing'."

"What is 'the thing'?" Luca asks.

Sonya taps the tip of her nose; they're giving away no secrets.

She shuffles out of the booth, Alice staying put,

"Right now, he's pretty much where you'll be, so count to twenty and you should be grand," Alice instructs her sister.

"Will do," she says, quickly heading through the front door and to the back of the building, so that they don't cross paths.

The rest of the group inside sit back down at the booth to make it look natural. On his way around, the guard notices that one of them is gone, but he figures she must be in the bathroom.

Sonya counts to twenty and, bang on time, the German rounds the corner. She drops down from the ladder, landing on his back. She digs the tips of her fingers into the pressure point between his neck and shoulders, and he immediately collapses to the ground.

"I'm gonna help her drag him in," Alice says, sliding out of the booth.

Luca and Mario follow her to the back door, where they find Sonya dragging the man by the bottom of his jeans.

"He's heavier than he looks!" she proclaims.

They sit the German in the booth behind them, and they proceed to talk about their proposal.

"So, what do you say?" Sonya asks.

Mario looks at Luca again. "Let me talk to The Don," he says, making his way to the staff area. "Keep an eye on these two." His brother nods in compliance.

"Ooh, 'The Don'... sounds cool." Alice smirks and raises her eyebrows at Sonya.

Luca beams. "That's our dad, Don Marco Fontana."

"Our dad's called Tim..."

"What's your name?" Alice asks him.

"Luca," he replies, "and you're Alice and Sonya." He tells them their own names.

"We prefer Al and Sonny. Only our relatives call us by our full, ugly names," Sonya explains.

"Al and Sonny," Luca repeats. "You would fit in well in an Italian Mafia family with names like that."

Calvino returns with the last two dishes. "This is all I'm doing for you, we need to save some for tomorrow's service."

"It'll do. Thanks, doll." Alice winks.

"Yeah, thanks for that, mate. Appreciated," Sonya adds, thrusting her fork through the middle of the lasagne.

Not long after, Mario returns. "My father wants to meet with you. We'll let you go home now, but we expect to see you at our residence tomorrow. Here's the address. Memorise it, then burn it."

"We will. Can we bag this lasagne up for the way home?" Sonya asks. The risotto has already disappeared.

"Where did that risotto go, did you drop it or something?" Calvino frowns.

"Yeah, down my throat," Sonya replies.

The Alfa picks them up again and drives them back to the shooting range, while the girls contently eat their lasagne out of Tupperware boxes with plastic forks in the back seats. Too busy eating to talk, the entire ride is enjoyed in silence.

Once the Alfa has driven off, they memorise the address, burn the note, and drive home like nothing even happened.

CHAPTER FIVE

The next day, early on a sunny Thursday morning, Alice wakes up, excited to meet her new 'family' tonight. She gets out of bed, brushes her teeth and hair and makes her way downstairs.

The low hum of her dad snoring, still in a tranquil slumber, travels through the landing. She silently roams through the house, making her way to the kitchen for a cup of tea. Once there, she spots her mum, Karen, sipping a brew and reading the newspaper on the patio outside. The morning sun provides her skin with a soft glow, and her spiky, short, blonde hair looks like a silky dandelion clock swaying in the cold breeze.

Alice goes to join her outside, mug in hand, the steam rising and dissipating into the late spring air.

"Morning, Mum." She smiles.

Karen looks up from her paper. She hadn't even heard Alice come outside. "Oh, good morning, little one."

"Anything newsworthy?" Alice asks, nodding at the newspaper.

"Never." She sighs. "How was shooting last night?"

"Good!"

"Did Sonya get a perfect bullseye again?"

"Of course she did."

Karen laughs. "She loves anything that she can do sitting down, that girl."

"I know, that's why I get her at fencing," Alice boasts.

"What are you two up to today, then?"

"We're going out for dinner tonight."

"Oh, where are you going?"

She smiles. "An Italian."

"Ooh, lovely."

"Yeah, can't wait," Alice says, taking a long sip of her brew, smirking, out of sight, into the mug.

Sonya pulls her Volkswagen up in front of a set of tall metal gates decorated with a large coat of arms. The small box next to the gate crackles and the audio comes through from the house.

"Who is it?" a thick Italian accent questions them.

"Sonny and Al Shelley, we're here to have dinner with the Fontana family."

Another crackle. "Ah, the German car caught me off-guard, I was ready to shoot you. Drive through." The gates slowly squeak open.

Sonny rolls her window back up and pulls a face at Al, as if to say 'close one'. They drive through a community of giant houses and mansions, until they reach the number they're looking for. The mansion is huge, and there's an elegant water fountain in the forefront. Tall windows and podiums frame the black front door that has a gleaming gold doorknocker in the shape of a lion's head.

They don't even get the opportunity to use it, as the door is swung open by Mario, who is dressed in an expensive fitted suit. He smiles at both of them as they walk across the drive towards the mansion,

"Welcome to our humble abode," he says, with his arms out wide.

"Have you been waiting all day to say that?" Alice laughs.

"Not all day." He winks.

They step inside and look around at all the beautifully elegant details of the mansion. It's more like an Italian heritage museum, with vintage marble statues and intricate paintings scattered along the walls and a giant mural on the ceiling.

"Whoa, it's mad in here."

"Look at the ceiling, it's like The Vatican!"

Mario laughs. "Glad you like it. Come through, dinner's almost ready. My family can't wait to meet you."

He leads them through to the dining room where the Fontanas are already sitting around the large table, chatting and picking at some stuzziccini.

Mario addresses the room. "Everybody, this is Al and Sonny Shelley."

All six diners stop talking and turn to observe their new guests. It's silent for a while as they size up the two new visitors.

The first to stand is Don Marco Fontana himself,

"It's a pleasure to meet the both of you. I am Don Marco Fontana," he introduces himself and shakes their hands. "This is my lovely family. My wife, Alessa."

The woman seated next to The Don rises to greet them. Her light grey hair is bunched on top of her head in a stylish, messy bun. An emerald green hummingbird hairpin keeps the short strands of hair neatly in place on the side of her head. She has a very elegant air about her; perhaps it's the high cheekbones.

She smiles and bows her head slightly. "Nice to meet you."

The Don continues, "I believe you have already met my sons, and my daughter Bella."

They all nod and wave from their seats.

"This is my youngest, Zeta." He identifies a young woman sitting with her arms crossed.

She has a brown pixie cut and heavy makeup to hide her many skin imperfections. She doesn't bother to smile; she just stares at Alice and Sonya with a straight face. The last thing she needs is two more girls to steal her spotlight from her dad, just like Bella has.

"Please take a seat, I'll go and get the dinner," Alessa states, gently pushing the girls towards the table before wandering off to the kitchen.

The girls look at the two empty seats at the end of the table, with Mario to the left and Bella to the right.

Sonya nudges Alice. "I'll take right."

Alice smirks back. "Fine by me."

"Did you find us alright?" Luca asks from across the table.

Sonya nods. "Yeah, no problems. Al's better with directions than I am."

"Yet we still manage to get lost on pretty much every night out we've ever been on." Alice laughs.

Mario smiles at them both. "That can be excused, though."

Alessa pushes a golden service trolley into the dining room. Every shelf is full to the brim with plates and tiny dishes. She puts the plates in front of Alice and Sonya first, then The Don, followed by her children.

"Would you like some wine?" she asks the girls.

They both say yes, with great enthusiasm. Once everyone is settled, they dig into their meal – homemade spinach and ricotta ravioli.

"This is the best ravioli I've ever had!" Alice praises.

Alessa beams. "Thank you, my dear."

"I've told you that before," Zeta says moodily.

Everyone looks at her, confused, making her blush with embarrassment.

Alessa turns to Alice and Sonya. "So, tell us a little more about yourselves. What is your family like?" she asks, changing the subject.

Sonya swallows her mouthful of ravioli and wipes her lips with her finger. "We get on well, I'd say. We don't argue very often, and we're always laughing."

"Our dad always takes us to do fun stuff, as well. We've had some really good trips away together," Alice adds.

"Have you ever been to Italy?" Luca asks them.

"We've been a couple of times. We went skiing in the Alps once, and then we went scuba diving in Parco Sommerso – that was absolutely amazing," Sonya reminisces.

"Have you seen Pompeii?" Mario asks.

Alice shakes her head. "No. I'd love to, though!"

"Maybe we could go one day." He smiles at her,

and then realises there are other people in the room, "All of us," he adds in a panic.

Her heart flutters momentarily before she regains her cool composure. "Maybe." She shrugs, with a smile.

"Tell us something about your family." Sonya asks the question to any one of the family members but The Don is the one who replies.

"Our families originated from Roma. Alessa and I moved to London in 1955. I hated the Southerners and so we moved to Manchester not long after. We built up our business and had our wonderful children." He looks at them all around the table. "You know, all of our names have a meaning?"

"Tell us!" Alice demands.

"My name, Marco, means warlike, and Mario means the God of war." He looks proudly at Mario, who gives him a respectful nod.

"Alessa means defender of mankind, which I think I do very well," The Don's wife says, with a smile.

"Is there a name that means 'defender of the ravioli'? 'Cause you also do that very well," Alice says, holding up a parcel on her fork before eating it.

Alessa laughs. "You think food comes first, above mankind?"

"Always."

"What does Luca mean?" Sonya asks.

"Bringer of light. We knew he was going to be the

brains of the family; as soon as he was delivered, he could count to ten." Don Marco laughs.

"I think we can all tell what Bella means," Sonya says to the owner of the name.

Bella looks at Sonya and smirks, looking her up and down once before turning back to her food.

"Ah, our beautiful Bella! The most perfect baby you would ever see. Big green eyes, long, sweeping eyelashes. She was a dream." Alessa smiles maternally.

"What about Calvino?" Alice asks.

"Don't," Calvino begs.

The Fontanas start to chuckle, even Zeta, who hasn't cracked a smile all evening.

"Have a guess." Bella laughs.

"Erm... Bald?" Alice predicts, just saying the first thing that came to mind when looking at him.

The whole family erupt into laughter, apart from Calvino.

"How did you get it?" Mario asks.

Alice can't help but laugh, too, despite feeling bad about it. "It was just a hunch."

"Italian babies are always born with black hair, but not this one," The Don says, pointing to Calvino. "He's never had a single strand."

"Yes, I have!" he objects.

"We used to call him Football Head, because he had eleven hairs on either side," Mario chokes out through laughter.

"That's why I just shave off what little hair I do have. I look like Gollum otherwise," Calvino explains, joining in on the jokes now.

"What does your name mean, Zeta?" Sonya asks.

"Last born." She gives a sulky scowl.

Everyone stops laughing and looks down at their plates.

Alice clears her throat quietly and places her cutlery down slowly, which prompts Alessa to stand up from her chair.

"Is everybody finished? I'll take the plates," she says, beginning to collect the dinnerware.

The girls begin piling their plates together for Alessa, which she is very thankful for; not even her own children are that courteous to her.

"Shall we have a break before dessert?" The Don announces to the table.

"Yes, please, I'm stuffed," the girls reply together.

"I would like to talk with you in my office, anyway. Come." He beckons, walking down to their side of the table. "Mario, you too."

The four of them enter the large office. Glass bookcases full of literature line the walls, momentarily separated by a drinks cabinet.

"Smoke?" Mario holds out a cigarette case for the girls to help themselves.

All four of them sit there in silence on the comfortable couches in the middle of the room, exchanging only puffs of smoke for a while.

The Don breaks the silence. "Mario told me about how you captured Holdis's guard outside the restaurant."

"Yeah, it was nothing." Alice shrugs.

Don Marco shakes his head. "I wouldn't call it nothing. Who knows what that man could have done to my family, or you two?"

"The plan to capture Holdis was more intricate than that one," Alice explains.

The Don asks her to detail the plan for him, which she does. He nods approvingly along with the story.

"Since I did not witness either of these endeavours, I wish to send you on a simple errand for me, to prove yourself." He looks from one to the other. "Are you in?"

"Yep," the girls say, in a creepy unison only twins could muster.

Mario frowns momentarily in shock. "Don't you want to know what the errand is first?"

"Doesn't matter. We want to be part of the family," Sonya explains.

The Don smiles, his cigarette clamped between his teeth like a cigar. "I'll tell you what it is, anyway, just so you know. I need you to smuggle twenty kilograms of cocaine into Amsterdam and drop it off with the Dutch Mafia family, the Van De Jaagers. I owe them for a load of marijuana they transferred to me last year."

"Sounds good." Alice nods.

"All expenses paid?" Sonya smiles cheekily.

The Don laughs. "Of course! You'll be there for three days, so as soon as the transaction is complete, you're free to do whatever you like."

The girls look at each other with wide eyes, then smile deviously, their eyes narrowing.

"This sounds amazing. When do we go?"

"How's tomorrow sound?" Mario asks.

They shrug. "Why not!"

The four return to the dining room just as Alessa plates up the dessert. Zeta is no longer at the table; the family had a discussion about Alice and Sonny and it all got too much for poor, forgotten Zeta.

"They're going to finish the business with the Van De Jaagers tomorrow," Don Marco says to his wife, pointing his fork at Alice and Sonya.

Alessa looks over at them, dressed in their casual clothes, colourful shirts and trousers, and no makeup. She clears her throat. "No offence, but we can't have you representing us when you look like that. Do you have any smarter clothes?"

The girls look at each other and then back to Alessa. "These *are* our smart clothes."

Alessa chuckles and shakes her head. "After

dessert, come to my studio, I'll measure you and we can make you something nice." She smiles.

"You might have to drop a coupla stone, I've eaten too much tonight!" Sonya laughs.

———

Alessa guides them through the spotless mansion, up the winding staircase and into a dress studio that looks like it was plucked straight from a high street in Milan. Handmade clothes cling to slim, headless mannequins and the walls are decorated with glistening, floor-length mirrors and colourful changing room curtains.

"Wow, this is amazing!" the girls gush.

Alessa smiles warmly. "Thank you, darlings. Let me get my tape measure."

She measures their waist, arm length and leg length, and jots it down on her little notepad. Once she's got all the measurements she needs, they move on to fabric and style.

"You want a skirt?" Alessa asks them.

They both pull a face in unison. "Trousers."

Sonya opts for a black felt, paisley suit with a blood red lining, and Alice goes for a green tartan suit with a red waistcoat. Alessa gets the materials ready and tells them that their suits will be waiting for them with their driver.

Once they return downstairs, the family

collectively walk the girls to the door to say goodbye for now.

"You will go to Amsterdam tomorrow as Alice and Sonya Shelley, and you will return as Al and Sonny Fontana, if all goes well," The Don says to them, after a brisk handshake and passing over the plane tickets and information enclosed in a manilla envelope.

"We won't let you down, Don Marco," they say, before hopping back into Sonya's VW.

Once they're out of the gates, they finally let go of the breaths they've been holding all night.

"What did you think of that then?" Sonya asks her sister.

"Pretty tense, but it was fun. They seem nice for a Mafia family."

She agrees. "They do."

"So, Amsterdam tomorrow as well! How excitiiing!" Alice sings.

"How are we going to hide this from Mum and Dad?"

Alice shrugs. "Just say it's another one of our spontaneous trips."

Sonya nods. "Good idea."

They return home and their parents are still waiting up for them.

THE DONS OF WARRINGTON

"How was dinner?" Karen asks them with a smile.

"Great! But we've got a confession to tell you..." Sonya starts.

Tim startles. "What is it?"

"We've spontaneously booked a holiday... for tomorrow."

"Tomorrow!" Karen shrieks, "How will you be ready?"

"Don't worry, Mum, everything's sorted." Alice smiles.

"You two, I don't know." Tim shakes his head.

"We'll be fine. It's only for a few days," Sonya reassures them.

They reluctantly let it go, and they all trail off to bed. Sonya and Alice secretly look through their abundance of information. Their flight departs at 5pm from Manchester, returning three days later. An apartment has already been booked out for them, ten minutes from the centre. The Van De Jaagers' address is provided in co-ordinates on a tiny piece of paper, along with the registration plate of the driver who'll be taking them to the airport and passing on the cocaine to them.

This 'errand' will make or break them in the Mafia world, but they aren't feeling the pressure one bit, just pure, fearless excitement.

CHAPTER SIX

Somehow, they manage to be ready in time for their 5 o'clock pick up. The driver is the same guy that kidnapped them a few nights ago, in his black Alfa Romeo. He's not as fun or as chatty as any of the other Fontana family members they've met. Alice imagines he gets on really well with miserable Zeta.

He pulls up in a private car park not far from the airport, and gathers together the bags of coke. He helps them to strap the bags against their skin and use their clothes tactically to conceal it as much as possible.

"I feel like you've done this before," Alice says to him, as he pulls her clothes around the bags.

"Many times," he mumbles quickly in his thick Italian accent.

"How long have you been with the family?" Sonya asks.

"Forever."

Sonya raises her eyebrows. "Cool."

He swiftly drops them off outside the terminal entrance and drags their duffle bags out of the boot, along with two black suit cover bags.

"Stay calm, and don't get caught. If you do, say nothing," he tells them in a hushed voice, before darting back into the car and speeding off.

They watch him drive off until they can't see him any longer,

"Shall we?"

"We shall."

Since they only have holdalls, they skip check-in and are herded into the line to security checks. They scan their boarding passes and wait in yet another line towards the x-ray scanners. This is the biggest hurdle they'll have to face. They decide to space themselves out, Sonya being a few people in front of Alice. Every now and again, Sonya turns back to look at Alice, just to see how she's doing. And she always returns the glance with a casual smile.

They're ordered to stand on a number at the conveyer belt to wait for a tray.

"Any boots, belts, electronics, jewellery need to go in the trays!" an impatient airport worker shouts at everyone in the line.

Sonya's heart drops suddenly as she places her

bag into one of the trays. *This is such a stupid thing to do*, she thinks, now starting to regret her decision to accept the job.

She stands in front of the metal detector, waiting for her turn. Alice now puts her things into a tray and, still a couple of people away, lines up to walk through the machine as well. She looks on in horror as the machine begins to beep loudly when Sonya walks through it. Both of them try to keep their cool and she is motioned over by a security guard.

It's Alice's turn to walk through, and she does so without triggering the machine. She stands near Sonya, who's being evaluated by the hand-held metal detector, but nothing goes off; she'll have to be searched.

"Sonya, is that you? I've not seen you in months!" Alice begins, hoping Sonya will get on board with the plan. "The last time I saw you was in hospital. How is the ringworm doing?"

Sonya looks at her, unamused. "Not great actually, Alice, that's why I'm here. It's the most infectious case they've ever seen, and there's a worm specialist in Amsterdam."

"Oh dear, that's not good, is it? Considering your entire family now has itchy worms... Is it curable?" she asks, taking a watch out of someone's tray and slyly passing it over to Sonya.

"Not yet."

"Shame," Alice says. "Well, see ya!" she chirps, collecting her items from the tray.

Sonya turns back to the security guard, who is now looking her up and down with a disgusted face.

"Oops, it could have been my watch!" Sonya says, holding up the timepiece.

"Put it in the tray and walk through again," the guard mutters.

Sonya walks through again and, as if by a miracle, the machine doesn't beep this time. She smiles at the guard and collects her belongings from the tray.

They regroup in the pub outside the gate,

"Worms?" Sonya says as she walks up to the table, getting a few odd stares from those that heard.

Alice burst into laughter. "Worked, didn't it? She wouldn't have touched you with a fifty-foot pole."

Sonya grabs her in a headlock. "You've got 'em now as well, so shut up."

Alice smoothes her hair down while Sonya gets settled on the other side of the table.

"We've got, like, ten minutes till the gates open, do you want a beer?" she asks.

"Go on then," Sonya agrees.

Alice returns from the bar with two pint glasses, sliding one across the table to Sonya.

"I should have known about the random beep, but there's no way for me to count which number it goes off on." Alice shakes her head.

Sonya takes a sip of beer, leaving a little white moustache above her lip. "Don't worry about it, we made it through."

"I suppose. I still need to be more thorough next time."

"Don't be so hard on yourself. We can blag our way through any problem."

They finish their drinks and make it onto their flight, and arrive in Amsterdam in less than an hour. At the airport, they're met by a driver holding a sign with the name *SHELLEY* written on it.

"How long are you here for?" he asks them, as he manoeuvres his way around cyclists, people and other cars.

"Just a few days," Sonya replies.

"Have you been before?"

"I've lost count of how many times I've been here." She laughs.

"It's a great place, isn't it?" he boasts.

"The best!" Alice sings from the back.

Just before they enter the street their apartment is on, they hit some road works which stop them for a short while.

"What's going on here?" Sonya asks.

"They are building a new road," he explains.

"Well, if there's one thing Amsterdam needs it's another road," Sonya jokes.

He doesn't get the sarcasm at first, and nearly unleashes a big rant about how there are *too many* roads. But then he laughs and nods. "Ha-ha, yes, yes. There are many roads."

He drops them off outside the apartment and wishes them a good holiday.

The owner of the apartment, who lives downstairs, comes to greet them at the door.

"Welcome to Amsterdam!" She beams at them both.

She takes them up the three flights of narrow stairs to the top floor of the building, where their room is situated. It's a small apartment with a minimal cooking area, a few comfy chairs in front of a TV, a bathroom, a little dining table and chairs and, behind a low dividing wall, a comfy-looking double bed. But best of all is the balcony, which includes a couple of lounge chairs, and an additional decked table and chairs.

"There's wine, cheese, juice, milk and other foods in the fridge for you. I bought you a loaf of seeded bread for you to enjoy as well," she tells them. "There are lots of places to go around here, there's some nice restaurants and bars further down the road. Some supermarkets and some lovely coffee shops."

This piques the girls' interest, until she continues, "They do amazing lattes and espressos around here." She smiles innocently.

They thank her for everything and with that, she

leaves them with the keys and returns to her own apartment downstairs.

As soon as they're alone, they begin ripping the bags of cocaine off their bodies, throwing them onto the dining table into a pile.

"You could have a good night with all of that," Alice says, admiring the powdery hill forming on the table.

Sonya laughs. "It's not for us, you know, Al."

They put all the coke together into another bag and stash it in the bathroom cabinet under the sink.

"So, we have all night to kill. What do you want to do?" Sonya asks.

All Alice has to do is raise an eyebrow and her sister knows exactly what she's thinking. They head out of the apartment after a change of clothes and go in search of a real coffee shop. The first one they come across looks more like a posh hotel lobby or some sort of weed palace. They use the vending machine to buy papers, filters and a grinder before heading to the desk. They buy two grams of Super Silver Haze and wander back to the apartment.

They roll two giant spliffs to celebrate their successful drug-smuggling adventure. They relax on the lounge chairs on their private balcony, looking up at the twinkly night sky, with the Big Dipper taking pride of place right above their heads. They smoke and chat all night, thinking nothing special of the weed until...

"We're gonna be out all day tomorrow, meeting the Van De Jaagers," Sonya says.

"Ooh! We can take a cheese sandwich," Alice offers.

This prompts Sonya into a storm of laughter, which is then reciprocated by Alice. They try to stifle their howls because of the numerous apartments that surround them, which are now full of sleeping families.

"I can't breathe!" Alice manages to push out in between her laughter.

"I don't even know why I'm laughing anymore, but it feels good," Sonya replies, which triggers another fifteen minutes of non-stop laughter.

They finally settle into a giggle, allowing themselves to breathe, which they hadn't done for a very long time. At one point they were genuinely scared for their lives, though dying of laughter was not the worst way to go, they decided.

Sonya sniggers slightly, thinking about how much they just laughed at nothing in particular.

"Don't, you're gonna make me start laughing again, and I don't think I'll be able to survive the next lot," Alice orders, taking deep breaths to prevent herself from another fit of cackling.

They finish smoking and promptly get into the soft bed that reminds them of something they'd see in their grandma's house, say goodnight, and both are out like a light as soon as they close their eyes.

The next morning, they wake up, have a spliff and devour the entire loaf of bread. (Solely used for jam on toast.) They throw the bags of coke into a duffle bag and put on their fancy new suits. Then they check the coordinates again, and set off to find the Van De Jaager mansion.

It turns out to be a longer walk than expected, but eventually, they find themselves at the entrance of a long, winding driveway that leads to a gigantic old-style mansion. It is clearly a lot more modest and reserved than the Fontanas', but you can still sense there is a vast fortune hidden inside.

"This must be it," Alice states.

"Let's go then," Sonya orders, already halfway down the drive.

This time, there is no handsome Italian to greet them at the door before they even get onto the doorstep. They wait outside the door for a second before Sonya rings the little black doorbell on the wall.

There is no sound arising from inside the mansion, apart from the annoying tune of the doorbell, taunting them as they wait impatiently. After what seems like forever, a crooked old man opens the door, mumbling something to himself.

"*Dag?*" He rasps. (Hello?)

"*Goedemorgen, we zijn hiervoor Mr Van De*

Jaager." Sonya smiles. (Good morning, we're here for Mr Van Dr Jaager.)

He grumbles again. "*Je mag binnen komen*," he reluctantly invites them in.

They thank him and slowly step inside. The house is beautiful and full of natural light. The walls are painted in vibrant colours and abstract pieces of art scatter the residence. As they walk through the house, laughter can be heard from some distant place.

He walks them to the backdoor. "*De familie is buiten*," (The family is outside), the old man tells them, so they head into the garden. Around a light-blue garden table sits a family of five. They're drinking a refreshing looking beverage full of fruit and bubbles, probably why they're all laughing so much. The older man of the group spots the girls walking towards them and his smiling face hardens when he gets a good look at them.

"Who are you?" he asks, standing up. The family has gone quiet now.

"I'm Sonny, this is my sister, Al. We're here under orders of Don Fontana."

He pauses, still looking very sceptically at them both. He then turns back to address his family, and lets out a big hearty laugh. "*Ze stuurden de Engelsen!*" (They sent the English!)

The rest of the family chuckle and go back to their conversation.

"Casper, you come with us. You might learn something." He grins at his oldest son.

He sniggers. *"Wat zou ik mogelijk kunnen leren van hun?"* He insults them in Dutch, thinking they won't understand. (What could I possibly learn from them?)

"Wij spreken Nederlands, trouwens," Alice states, deadpan. (We speak Dutch, by the way.)

The father and son look at each other quickly and then back at the girls.

"Heren, wij zijn hier met een reden." (Gentlemen, we're here for a reason.)

Sonya nods along. *"Ja, wees professioneel."* (Yeah, be professional.)

The older man clears his throat. *"Natuurlijk."* (Naturally.)

"Shall we go and do business then?" Alice asks, facing towards the house.

The man gathers himself again. "Yes, let's," he says, showing them to the office that's only around the corner from the backdoor.

His office is very minimalistic, but colourful red bookcases home an abundance of book spines from every author you could think of. His desk is an ash grey colour that's almost blue and the sofas that form a horseshoe in the middle of the room are orange, yellow and green respectively.

Don Van De Jaager takes a seat behind his desk,

his blond, thinning hair reflecting the sunlight pouring in from the floor-length window behind him. He's wearing a light green bowling shirt and white trousers, making the girls feel like they've overdressed.

His son, Casper, is in equally smart casuals, plain white shirt and matching father-and-son white trousers. Must have been 2for1, Sonya thinks. His hair, the same colour as his clothes, swoops straight down and sticks to his forehead, making it look like he's wearing a helmet made of soft snow.

Sonya unbuttons her blazer and takes a seat and Alice settles down next to her. She flicks up the back of her blazer to sit down, her elbows perched on her knees.

"You're like a pair of middle-aged businessmen," Casper says, an attempt at an insult.

"We are business, man," Alice says, hoping to ignore him for the rest of the meeting.

Sonya, however, wishes to rile him up. "You look like ABBA's love child."

"*Ze zijn Zweedse, idioot.*" He scowls. (They are Swedish, idiot.)

"You're an *idioot*!" she retaliates.

"Both of you, shut up," Mr Van De Jaager interrupts.

Sonya relaxes back on to the couch and Casper shakes his head angrily.

He takes a deep breath, "My name is Aart. My son, Casper." He points dismissively. "What did you say your names were again?" he asks, seeming distracted.

"Al and Sonny."

"Fontana?"

"No, we're not part of the family."

He frowns. "Why are you here then?"

"Repaying a favour," Alice says, eager to just get the deal done.

"Ah, so this must be our premium delivery. Also a favour." He winks.

Sonya gets up and puts the duffle bag onto his desk. "I believe so."

Aart begins opening the bag and Casper rushes over to get a glimpse as well. You can tell there is a little bit of resentment between the two as Aart leans away from him slightly.

"Is it all there?" Casper shouts accusingly.

Aart rolls his eyes briefly. "Yes, it's all there."

"I don't know, Dad. *Ik vertrouw ze niet.*" He questions their credibility, saying he doesn't trust them.

Aart bangs his fist on the desk abruptly. "Leave us, Casper! You're no help to me."

His son straightens up, still in shock. He looks around slowly until his eyes meet the girls again and his face twists into a glare. "Fine," he spits. He doesn't take his eyes off the girls until the door closes on his face.

"I love him, but he can be so annoying sometimes," Aart says, rubbing his forehead with his palm.

Sonya smiles. "Our parents say that about us, too."

He laughs. "I'm sure you're not that annoying. You seem like a pair of smart-headed girls... I'm sorry for underestimating you earlier, it's just that when a man like Don Fontana sends a couple of young girls to do his business, it's unexpected."

"That's the point." Alice shrugs. "But don't worry about it, we get it all the time."

"When did you learn to speak Dutch?" he asks them.

"We started teaching ourselves about two months ago," Sonya remembers.

He looks shocked. "Two months and you know all of that?"

"We pick languages up pretty quickly."

"I'll say! What others do you know?"

"All the European languages, all the Scandinavian ones, Latin, Hebrew, Mandarin, Afrikaans... I could go on forever," Sonya lists.

"Wow... You're both extraordinary, aren't you?" He shakes his head in astonishment.

Alice blushes at the compliment. "That's why we're here, Don."

"How much longer are you here for?" he asks them.

"We leave tomorrow morning."

He opens the top drawer of his desk and throws two little bags of cocaine to them. "Take this as a peace offering. You can do with it as you like... Have fun." He laughs.

"I'm sure we will." They laugh back, pushing the bags into their pockets.

"Would you care to stay a little longer? I can introduce you to the rest of my family."

Alice nods. "But only if I can have a glass of whatever you were drinking outside."

"Of course, it is my wife's speciality drink!"

The three of them head back into the garden. Unfortunately, Casper is there, too.

"Family! This is Al and Sonny. Girls, this is family." He introduces them all awkwardly.

"Hi, family!" Alice smiles.

His wife stands up to greet them. "Hello girls, my name is Skylar," she says in a beautifully soft voice. She gives off the same vibe as Alessa, kind, but cruel if you cross her.

"That's a lovely name for a lovely woman," Sonya compliments her.

She smiles warmly. "Are you joining us?"

"If that's okay. We'd like to get to know you all," Alice replies.

"Of course. Abel!" She calls to the old man who let the girls in. He appears at the backdoor. *"Twee stoelen, alsjeblieft,"* she asks politely. (Two chairs, please.)

He returns moments later, carrying two deck chairs under his arms. He unfolds them and places them around the table.

"Dank je wel," the girls thank him before sitting down.

Skylar pours them a glass of whatever is in the ice-cold pitcher. Alice watches the juicy pieces of fruit fall into the glass with a splash.

"Hi, I'm Jelle." A young man with curly blond hair smiles at them both. His perfectly clear skin and crystal blue eyes dazzle in the mid-morning sun.

"I'm Bente." The only daughter of the family introduces herself. She seems reserved and abrupt but not entirely unfriendly. She has flawless, glowing skin as well, and beautiful big, blue eyes to match the rest of the family's.

"And you must be Casper!" Sonya says to him.

He rolls his eyes and ignores them both, opting instead to stare blankly at his phone screen.

"Sorry, I don't know what's gotten into him today." Skylar motions to Casper.

"Not to worry, he's probably just going through the moody teenager stage." Sonya smiles condescendingly at him.

"I'm twenty-five." He scowls.

Alice pulls a 'yikes' face. "It happens to some a bit later on, I suppose."

The rest of the family laugh at their teasing. They must know he deserves it.

"You know, all of our children's names have a meaning behind them?" Aart begins, sounding familiar.

"Is that a Mafia family thing? Because Don Fontana told us the same."

He laughs. "Perhaps."

"What do they mean, then? Enlighten us."

"Well, Casper means 'king of the treasure.' Jelle means 'sacrifice', and Bente means 'brave'," he explains.

"Oh, that's interesting! Do Aart and Skylar have a deeper meaning, too?" Sonya quizzes them further.

"Aart means 'strong', Skylar means 'shelter.'" He smiles at his wife, taking hold of her hand.

Alice smiles. "They're all very nice, and fitting names for you all."

"Thank you, my dear." Don Van De Jaager smiles back at her.

"*Slijmbal*." Casper mutters under his breath. (Slimeball.)

"Shut it, *mammalucco*," she replies, calling him 'stupid' in Italian so only Sonya would understand.

Alice finishes her drink in two big gulps, tipping

the fruit at the bottom of the glass into her mouth. "Perfect," she says with a gasp.

Skylar chuckles. "I'm glad you liked it."

"You've got a lovely house as well. The grounds look huge," Sonya says.

"Jelle, Bente, why don't you show them around before they go?" Skylar insists.

They agree to, leaving Casper alone with his parents, to be lectured about respect and courtesy.

The group slowly wander around the grounds, Bente pointing something out every so often for them to look at. Jelle wanders closer to Alice and whispers to her, out of earshot of Bente, "It was so cool when you stood up to my brother, he's such a dick."

"I've definitely met worse."

He raises his eyebrows. "I don't think I have."

"That's because you live with him."

"I suppose. I can't wait to move out. Even though it's legal and it's basically our whole business, my parents don't like me smoking weed." He rolls his eyes.

"'Don't get high off your own supply'?" she asks.

He titters. "That, and they want me to fully concentrate on the business. But I know I can do both; I have been."

"What are you two whispering about?" Bente trudges over, Sonya trailing behind.

"Just because you can't hear it doesn't mean we're whispering," Jelle snarls at his sister.

"Whatever. I'm going back to the house," she says, stomping her way back through the garden.

"She prefers Casper to me, for some reason... Shall we smoke? We have a great little treehouse down here."

"Sounds great!" Sonya agrees.

They start towards the treehouse, which is situated on the forest edge at the far side of the garden.

"This was built when we were younger. Cas was still a massive dick back then, maybe even more so than he is now."

Sonya recoils slightly. "God, I don't even want to imagine it."

"I know. I've lost count of how many times he's kicked me out of this treehouse." He gives a bittersweet laugh.

They climb up the rotting wooden ladder and crawl into the small room, which is full of old toys and comics. There is one chair in the corner, but the floor looks much more inviting.

Jelle pulls a spliff from his pocket and lights it quickly. "So, what are you going to do for the rest of your trip?" he asks them.

"We don't have any plans. We'll probably just go out for a drink later and then get to bed; our flight is quite early tomorrow."

He nods slowly. "Cool. There's so much to do here, you never get bored."

"I know, we love it; it's like our second home."

He smiles. "Well, next time you're here, we'll have to meet up!"

"Definitely! And if you're ever in Manchester, we'll show you around."

"Sounds great!" he says excitedly.

They pass the spliff around, talking about their families and where they come from. They swap numbers before struggling back down the ladder. They rejoin the rest of the family for a second, just to say goodbye, before they're seen off at the door by Aart, Skylar, Jelle and little old Abel.

The two of them take a casual stroll back to the apartment; Alice took in all the scenery on the way here, and so she manoeuvres them back purely through visual cues.

"So, Al... Our first mission has been a success!" Sonya says.

"It has been. It was fun and all but still not as actiony as I'd like," Alice complains.

Sonya laughs. "I repeat: it's only our *first* mission! We'll get something bigger and better next time, now we've proven ourselves."

"I hope so."

Just down the road from their apartment, they spot an English pub, styled on Newcastle FC.

"Shall we just have a quick drink in here before we go home?" Sonya asks.

Alice agrees and they step up to the bar inside the small building. Old men of all nationalities, but mostly English and Dutch, prop up the bar while they watch football on TV. The owner appears from a door behind the bar. His eyes are wide and his movements erratic.

"Sorry about that, gurls, I've just had toow lynes a cowk in the bogs!" he declares, in his thick Geordie accent.

"Wow!" they say in shock.

"That's good to know!" Sonya laughs.

"What can I get for ya?" he asks, finally doing his job.

"Can we have a bottle of white, please?" Sonya orders.

"It's actually cheapah ta buy it by the glass."

A guy at the bar laughs at his honesty.

"We'll have two large glasses then," Sonya says, going with it.

They get their drinks and sit at one of the little tables outside. A pint of beer is sitting alone on the table next to them and soon enough, its owner reappears. A short Indian girl with a pixie cut, dressed in an Amsterdam University hoodie, plonks herself down on the bench attached to the wall.

The girls get talking to her and they find out that

her name is Ravi, and she is studying to be some sort of rocket scientist for NASA.

"That's crazy! You must be so smart," Alice gushes in amazement.

"I was, but being here is hard, you know? You go to a party, you drink, then they're passing spliffs around. My head falls off and I don't wake up for days. This is every night!" Ravi explains.

Sonya laughs and takes a sip of wine. "You'll have to build up your tolerance."

"Well, there's a festival on tonight that I could go to, but I have no money so I was planning on sneaking in or something."

The girls look at each other, smirking. "We could get you in."

"Really?" Ravi booms in excitement.

Alice nods. "Just tell us where it is and we'll find a way."

Ravi pulls up the destination on her phone and hands it to Sonya,

"You're better off giving it to Al, she's the organiser," she says, passing it along.

Alice flicks through the pictures, zooming in, zooming out and turning the phone upside down. It only takes a couple of minutes before her plan starts taking shape,

"This is going to be so easy!" She smiles triumphantly.

The three of them finish their drinks whilst they

wait for their taxi. It drops them off a few miles away from the festival. They thank the driver and Alice leads them through a forest.

"Where the hell are we going?" Sonya asks impatiently.

Alice rolls her eyes. "Just wait a second and you'll see!"

She turns to look at Ravi and Sonya with a big smile on her face. She gives them a quick raise of the eyebrow before she parts the mass of twigs and bushes that block their path. Behind it is a view like no other. A beautiful blue lake ripples violently in the wind. Across it is another little island, full of partygoers and DJs. The music blasts through the air, making it sound like they're already in the festival.

Sonya looks on, unimpressed. "And how are we supposed to get over there?"

"Boat," Alice responds.

"What boat?"

"This boat." She points to a dark wooden rowing boat beached on the sand bank.

Sonya nods. "Alright. Let's do it then."

The three of them climb into the boat, Sonya picking up the oars to row.

"Thanks for helping me get here, guys, I would never have thought of this!" Ravi praises, in her thick Indian accent.

"No worries, it's fun anyway," Alice tells her, while sitting at the front of the boat, navigating.

"How did you know this boat was here?" Ravi asks.

"I could see it on the satellite image. Must have been here for a while."

They swiftly make it across the lake – kayaking has always been the girls' strongpoint – and pile out of the boat, onto the sandy landscape.

"I can't believe I'm actually here! I can't thank you enough!" Ravi gushes.

Sonya smiles at her. "Go and have fun, mate."

Ravi beams a full smile before running off into the festival, turning back a few times to wave goodbye to the girls.

Sonya turns to her sister. "What do we do now then? Stay?"

Al shrugs. "Might as well."

First stop is the bar for a bottle of wine, swiftly followed by a trip to the Portaloos for a wee and a key. Then they join the rest of the party, stopping off at every stage they walk past. It takes about five seconds in each crowd for someone to come up to them offering drugs. They say no every time; they already have the highest-grade stuff in their pockets.

After hours of dancing, they lie down on a riverbank and are soon surrounded by a hoard of people from all over the world. They share a spliff with a couple of backpacking Australians and spend the majority of the night chatting with a group of Dutch friends. They drink and do drugs all night, to the point where they can hardly stand up or control where they're walking.

At the end of the night, when everyone gets ushered out onto the street, they stumble towards a taxi rank and give him the address of the apartment. When they arrive, Sonya fumbles with the key, desperately trying to get it into the lock. She does eventually, but the biggest task is climbing the three narrow staircases without waking up the old tenant. They have a little spliff to get them to sleep, and they do just that as soon as their heads hit the soft, crinkly pillow.

At 9 o'clock the next morning, they empty the bin in their room and return the keys to the landlady. Sonya has thrown up a few times due to her hangover, but Alice feels better than ever; their first assignment is finally done and they're ready for the next, more difficult mission.

They sleep for the entire hour-long flight and sleepily trudge through Manchester airport towards the arrivals gate.

"How are we even gonna get home? Have they sorted us a driver?" Sonya yawns.

Alice looks around at all the name signs held up by drivers who are standing around like statues, waiting for their cargo. She spots the familiar face of the Alfa Romeo driver, the names *Al and Sonny Fontana* scrawled across the paper held in front of his chest.

So, The Don wasn't lying. They left Manchester as Alice and Sonya Shelley, and have returned as fully-fledged members of the Fontana crime family!

CHAPTER SEVEN

On the drive home, Al sits on the back seat checking her phone. There is a message from her dad: *You're not too busy to go to Wacky's with your dad tonight, are you? X*

She smiles at her phone, and replies *Course not, we'll be home soon x*, and switches her phone off.

The driver looks through the rear view mirror at her and then at Sonny in the passenger seat. "The Don received a call from the Van De Jaagers. Aart had only good things to say about you both."

"That's great." Sonny smiles.

"He wants to know if you are available for a meeting tonight?"

"We can't tonight. We have training on Sundays," Al butts in, before Sonny can agree to it.

Sonny nods slowly, thinking. "Oh yeah, that's right... We can do tomorrow, though."

"I'll let him know."

The car fills with silence for a few moments.

"I'm sorry but I don't even know your name," Al says, leaning into the front of the car.

"Lorenzo," he mumbles.

Al puts her hand on his shoulder. "Nice to finally get to know you, Lorenzo. There's no need to kidnap us anymore."

He chuckles and shakes his head. "I should apologise for that. It's just my job."

"Don't worry about it, we know," Sonny reassures him.

Lorenzo drops them off around the corner from their house and bids them farewell.

They're greeted at the front door by both of their parents, who give them a giant hug and a kiss on the cheek.

"How was your holiday?" Shelley asks them.

The girls smile at each other. "It was fun."

"The Wacky is booked for five o'clock, so you've got time to chill out first."

"Thanks, Dad," they say, before heading off to bed for a lie down.

Sonny lies fast asleep in her room. It's covered in purple wallpaper and her bed sits in the middle of the back wall. She is awoken by a tiny noise from outside her room. She opens one eye, but sees nothing and so shuts it again, attempting to go back to sleep. A mere few seconds later, she opens her eyes to see Al's face centimetres from hers. Sonny jumps back and puts her hand on her viciously beating heart.

"Bloody hell, you scared me. I didn't even hear you come in." Sonny breathes heavily.

Al laughs. "I'm practicing my stealth. That one floorboard in the landing buggers me up every time, though."

"Well, can you practice it on someone else?"

"I only came to tell you we're going in, like, ten minutes," Al says, as she heads out the door.

Sonny groans. "Ugggh, alright. I'll get ready now."

Al dances down the top few stairs before she spots her dad standing underneath her in the hall. She watches him for a minute to see if he's noticed her. He hasn't.

She quietly climbs up onto the railing, perching steadily. She counts down from three and jumps off, landing on her dad's back. She grabs him and pretends to strangle him from behind.

He thrashes around for a minute, making Al feel

like she's on a rodeo bull. Then he starts to laugh, finally realising what's going on,

"Alice, I could have killed you then! You can't keep doing stuff like that." He tries to lecture her without laughing.

She slides off his back. "I coulda killed you, man!" she mocks him. "You wouldn't have had the chance, mate."

"Come 'ere!" he shouts, dragging her into a headlock.

Al tries to grab his legs to get him onto the floor, but he picks her up sideways and gently 'throws' her onto the ground. He pins her arms down and starts counting to three slowly. "One-ahhh, two-ahhh..."

Before he gets to 'three', he loosens his grip so her arms lift off the floor, but he pins them straight back down, starting the countdown all over again,

"A-one-ahhhh, a-two-ahhhh." She lifts them up again.

"One-ahhh, two-ahhhh."

Sonny wanders down the stairs now, watching the scene unfold over the banister.

"Sonny, help!" Al laughs.

She snorts. "No."

"One-ahhh, two-ahhhh, thhhhrrrrreeeeee-ahhhhhhh. I win!" he says, finally letting her get up off the floor.

Al dusts herself off. "Unfair advantage."

"Just get in the car," he tells them, picking his keys up off the table.

They pull up into the empty Wacky Warehouse car park, thinking that even a place filled with fun can look gloomy on the outside. The Post-it note on the door says 5/9, indicating which shoe pockets hold their state-of-the-art static socks that help the girls grip to the plastic walls.

Shelley swings the doors open and they wander down the steps into the playing area.

"Slush, anyone?" Shelley jokes, as the girls replace their shoes with the socks hidden in pouches 5 and 9.

"I know you're joking but I'm defo having one before we go," Sonny tells him.

"Right, go on, then. Let's see what you've got," Shelley demands.

Al looks at Sonny over her shoulder, slowly edging towards the multi-coloured staircase leading into the giant, soft play area. Sonny stands up, ready to chase her.

Al dashes up the stairs, taking three steps at a time. Sonny barely gets to the first step before she's lost sight of her sister,

"You always get me on the stairs!" she shouts.

The lights illuminating the play area are dim, so their vision is slightly impaired as they run through the obstacles. Sonny quietly stalks through the hanging punchbags decorated with images of the

Wacky's mascots. Suddenly, one of them gets pushed into her, and she sees Al run out of that area, across the thickly netted, very narrow bridge.

"Sonny's gonna get ya!" Sonny shouts, as she pursues her quickly.

The slide is straight ahead, and Sonny knows that Al will be throwing herself down there, so she takes a detour, dropping through the holes in the floor that bring you out on the bottom level – just outside the ball pit that homes the big red slide.

Al dives straight through it, flying head-first down the slide. It takes all of her might not to sing "Wheeeee!" on her way down – she must be silent and stealthy.

As she reaches the ball pool, she spots Sonny clambering in through the small entrance. Al screams playfully and spins around to climb back up the slide, but Sonny grabs her by the ankle and tries to pull her back down.

Al's hands screech against the plastic slide as she desperately tries to push herself up.

"Come here, you little bugger!" Sonny shouts, also putting all of her strength into pulling her down.

Eventually, Al's strength deteriorates and the girls gently slide down into the ball pool. They both lie down, breathing heavily, surrounded by the colourful plastic balls.

"Told you I'd get you," Sonny pants.

"You got lucky," Al replies.

Sonny lets out as much of a laugh as she can muster. "Nothing lucky about that strategical capture."

Al picks up one of the balls near her hand and launches it at Sonny, who sits up after the impact. She sees Al still lying down.

"Was that you?"

"No," Al says, with her eyes closed now.

A light red ball flies into Al's eyelid and she recoils, holding her eye. "Ow! Not the eyes, I need those!"

"Oh, shut up."

Before they can fight anymore, a big fumbling sound travels down the slide. Al moves out of the way of the lip of the tunnel and Shelley appears, feet first, into the ball pit as well.

"Took your time," Al quips.

"Who won?"

"Me!" Sonny sings.

Shelley claps his hands together once. "Your turn to chase Sonny now, then."

Sonny darts out of the ball pool as soon as this is said, but Al continues to stand in the rainbow puddle, just watching where her sister is running to. She looks at her dad and smiles.

"This is gonna be my record time, I bet you."

"Go on, girl," he urges her.

She wades through the balls and climbs out. Looking around, she can tell Sonny isn't on the ground floor anymore. Al runs at the wall and places one static foot firmly at head height, before pushing off and hoisting herself through the netted platform above.

She keeps low to the ground, looking through the gap-filled walls into the other rooms in the play area. She spots some movement travelling past the bubble window in one of the tube tunnels. She heads for the tunnel exit, slipping through narrow gaps in the big apparatus.

Sonny crawls as quietly as possible through the yellow tunnel, peeking out of the windows every now and again, seeing nothing. She laughs to herself. *Al will never find me.* She is only a few crawls away from the end of the tunnel when, from above, Al's head appears and she smiles at her upside down,

"*Heeeere's* Ali!" she shouts.

Sonny has nowhere to go, it's useless crawling backwards. She sighs and admits defeat.

"I've got her, Dad!" Al shouts across the play area.

"ONE MINUTE!" echoes through the room; he has no idea where they are.

Al begins to celebrate, jumping off the top of the tunnel and doing a little dance to herself.

"Is that the new record?" Sonny asks, flopping out of the tunnel onto the soft floor.

"It is indeed, Sonya," she teases.

Sonny picks herself up. "We'll see how long that lasts." She smiles.

They meet up with their dad near the shoe pouches again, placing the socks back into numbers 5 and 9.

"You did well tonight, girls. You've improved loads since last week," Shelley praises them.

"Does that mean we can get a Slush, then?" Sonny smiles.

Shelley tuts. "Go on then. But make me one, too."

"I'll have a mixed, thanks, hun." Al smirks.

Sonny backhands her on the arm, but pours her a mixed Slush regardless. They drive home slurping away at the sugary goodness, listening and singing along to their favourite songs.

CHAPTER EIGHT

Monday morning, Tim Shelley leaves the house with a piece of toast dangling from his mouth, briefcase in one hand and his travel mug and car keys in the other. Karen waves him off through the living room window before returning to the kitchen.

She cooks up two bacon sandwiches, one with brown sauce and one with red, as well as two cups of tea. She carries them upstairs on a little handheld tray. Karen pushes Sonny's bedroom door open with her foot and the smell of bacon is enough to wake Sonny from her slumber.

She distributes the ketchup-covered sandwich and a brew onto the bedside table and they have a quick chat before she goes to take Al's to her room. When she opens the door, Al is already up, sitting at her desk below the window. She quickly spins around on her chair and spots her mum standing in the doorway.

"What are you doing up already?" Karen asks her.

"Dad woke me up when he left, so I thought I would get some work done."

Karen steps into the room and places the tray down on the bed. "What work?"

"Just for the start of uni. It's about deception detection," she explains, showing Karen the notes spread across the desk.

"Hmm, so you'd know if I was lying to you?" Karen grins.

"Test it out."

"I've put ketchup on your bacon butty," she lies.

"Now I know that's definitely a lie! You wouldn't disrespect me like that."

Karen laughs softly. "You got me. I'm going shopping with Flo in Manchester, so I won't be at home today. Will you be alright?"

Al smiles. "I think we'll survive."

"Alright, hun. I'll see you tonight," she says, and kisses Al on the head.

Not long after Karen has left, the house phone rings. Al answers it.

"Hello?"

"Al?" an Italian voice rings through the phone.

"Yeah. I would try to guess which one you were,

but you all sound too similar, so you might as well just tell me."

"It's Mario. You and Sonny sound exactly the same too, you know." He laughs.

Sonny hears the talking from upstairs and comes to join Al in the front room to see who is calling. 'Who is it?' she mouths.

"Oh, Mario! To what do I owe this pleasure?" Al says with emphasis.

Sonny picks up the other phone in the kitchen to join the call.

"I was just... Is there someone else on the line?" he quizzes.

Al and Sonny look at each other through the doorway, both with a phone held to their ear.

"Me," Sonny quips.

"Al?" a now very confused Mario asks.

"No, that was Sonny this time," Al says.

"So, you're both on the phone now?"

"Yeah," the girls say at the same time, in exactly the same way.

Mario sighs down the phone. "This is just confusing. When shall I schedule this meeting for?"

"Why don't you come round to ours? Nobody will be home until tonight," Sonny suggests.

"Alright, it will only be a quick meeting, anyway. I'll speak to The Don. Expect us any time, and we have a little present for you both."

"Sounds great! See you soon," Sonny quips down

the phone, before putting it back on the charging base.

"'Bye, Mario," Al says, before hanging up as well.

"Ooh, 'bye Mario! Love you!" Sonny teases her sister.

Al laughs. "Shut up. We need to get ready."

———

About an hour later, there's a knock at the door. Sonny opens it to be presented with The Don, Mario and Luca.

"Hi, guys, come in!" she says, stepping back from the doorway to let them in.

The Don takes a quick look around the house before shaking the girls' hands and praising them for their work in Amsterdam. They all take a seat outside in the patio area, smoking cigarettes and drinking coffee.

"Luca, hand them their presents." The Don beckons to him.

Luca dives into a giant bag by the side of the chair and pulls out two large, flat boxes. He checks the name tags and hands one to Sonny and one to Al.

"Ooh, I wonder what it is!" Al smiles excitedly.

They each slide the lid off their box and unfold the tissue paper inside to uncover a new handmade suit.

Al's is a navy and maroon striped suit with a

matching waistcoat, paired with matching trousers and a custom-made, white, high-neck shirt.

"This looks amazing!" She beams, holding up the blazer.

Sonny's is an electric blue floral suit that has black trousers and a custom-made, black, button-down shirt.

"Whoa, I love it!"

They both say "Thank you," and the Italians brush it off as nothing,

"Alessa loves to make new suits all the time," The Don waves his hand around, "and anyway, they are to show our gratitude. Not everyone would have done what you did."

"It was nothing, really," the girls say bashfully.

"Don Van De Jaager called me. He said he underestimated the situation at first, but was soon aware of your capabilities. Just as I did." He blows out a big cloud of smoke. "We have a lot of respect for each other, he and I."

Al nods. "He seems nice. Not sure I can say the same about Casper, though. Thought he was supposed to be a friendly ghost?"

The Don shakes his head. "He has a lot of trouble with that boy. Some drug busts that should never have happened."

"He didn't tell us about that," Sonny says.

"Anyway," Luca interrupts, "we want to talk to you about your new assignment."

"What is it?" Sonny asks.

The Italians look at each other sceptically.

Mario clears his throat and takes a steadying breath. "It's the favour that your dad wouldn't do for us."

"We need you to kill Detective Leaver," Luca states, throwing them a manila folder that holds information about Leaver.

"He knows we tipped your dad off about Holdis. Now he's coming for us, hard. He has to be eliminated as soon as possible," The Don explains slowly.

The girls shoot a quick glance at each other before sliding the folder off the table and flicking through it.

"We have bigger things to concentrate on at the minute, so this one will be left to you two. Do you think you can handle it?" The Don asks, tapping his thumb on his chin.

"Of course," Sonny answers, before they have even discussed it.

"I will be available on this number if you need any help with the planning," Luca says, handing Al a business card.

She just nods and looks at the card silently.

"Well, we'll leave you to conjure up your plan. Come and see us at the house when the assignment is complete," The Don tells them, standing up from the chair.

"I'll see you out!" Sonny says, running ahead to open the front door.

Al shakes the hands of The Don and Luca before they head for the door, leaving her with Mario outside.

"Is everything okay?" he asks worriedly.

She nods. "I've just never killed anyone before."

He smiles warmly and puts his hands on her shoulders. "And you don't have to. Sonny seems up for it, you just do the planning. Luca's never killed anyone, either, but he's planned hundreds of hits."

"Hmm." She nods. "Okay."

He holds out his hand for a handshake. Al grins and their hands meet firmly. "Very formal," he says, quirking an eyebrow.

Once they're out the door, the Fontanas turn back to the girls to wish them luck.

"Where's Bella, by the way?" Sonny asks them.

"She's on a mission of her own," The Don tells her, as they begin to walk away.

They wave goodbye to them and shut the door.

"Ooh, where's my Bella? My beautiful Bella!" Al teases Sonny this time.

Sonny rolls her eyes and snatches the folder out of Al's hand. She flicks through the pages, which include a profile on Detective Leaver.

"So, he works with Dad," Sonny says as she scours the pages.

"Are you alright with killing someone?" Al raises an eyebrow at her sister.

Sonny shrugs. "It's just a job."

"I'll leave it to you then," Al tells her. "I'll start the planning." She takes the folder out of her sister's hands and trudges upstairs to her desk.

Sonny chills out in the front room while she waits for Al to conjure up a plan.

An hour after she went upstairs, Al returns. "I've got it! And it's going to be fun." She smiles.

"Go on, impress me," Sonny says, giving Al her full attention now.

"So... I snooped on Dad's computer – don't tell him. It turns out Detective Leaver has booked this week off, he's on an island in Wales with his family. This is where we'll get him."

"In front of his family? Oh, Al, you are cruel!" Sonny jokes.

She rolls her eyes. "Not in front of them! But they will be there. We need to get a handgun with a silencer, as well."

"The Fontanas will have something. We need one that can't be traced so there's no point in getting it from the gun range."

Al agrees. "I know. I'll send them a text and see what they can do for us."

"But a road trip to Wales, though!" Sonny sings in excitement.

"Ha-ha, buzzing," Al jokes, half ironically.

The Shelley family sit around the dinner table that night, chowing down on their usual Monday meal. Detective Shelley is starting to look more and more stressed and worn out as every night passes. He pushes a limp piece of broccoli around his plate, staring at it thoughtfully.

"It's not like you to not clear your plate, Tim," Karen quizzes him.

He snaps out of his trance. "Sorry, hun. I've been getting a lot of stick at work."

"About what?" Al asks, with a mouthful of chicken.

"Holdis, mainly. There's one detective who's taken it really badly, he's making my life hell at work," he explains.

Sonny quickly looks up from her plate. "What's his name?"

"Leaver." He sighs.

Al and Sonny throw a quick glance at each other.

"Want us to beat him up for you?" Al offers.

Shelley laughs. "Don't worry, girls. He'll get what's coming to him."

Sonny raises her eyebrows and stares down at her plate again.

The phone begins to ring abruptly.

"I'll get it!" Al shouts, dashing out of the dining room.

Karen looks on in shock. "What's gotten into her?"

"Hello?" Al answers in the living room.

"Hey, it's Mario."

Al walks outside with the phone. "You need to start ringing us on something better than the house phone."

"I know, I know. We've got your pistol, equipped with a silencer. You need to come round and give it a test run. *And*, we've got you both an untraceable mobile that we'll contact you through, from now on."

"Sounds great! Thanks so much." She smiles at the phone.

"No problem. You can come tonight or tomorrow. I'll see you soon."

"Okay, see you tonight," and she hangs up the call.

Al walks back into the dining room.

"Who was it?" Karen asks.

"Mitherer." Al shrugs, throwing a look to Sonny.

"Why do they always ring when you're having dinner?" Karen rolls her eyes.

"God knows..." Al shakes her head. "Do you fancy going shooting tonight, Sonny?"

"Sure."

"Don't end up as assassins, you two." Tim laughs.

"We're called 'Justice Warriors' actually, Dad."

"Well, whatever you call it. Why don't you join the police force?" he suggests.

The girls pull a face at each other. "Don't think so." They laugh.

"Why not?" he asks, slightly offended.

"Boring, innit?" Sonny shrugs.

"No! You can help your dad beat the Mafia families," Karen butts in.

"I'd rather be part of the Mafia." Al smiles cheekily.

Karen gasps. "Don't say that!"

"She was only joking, dear," Tim reassures her.

They finish their meal and Al and Sonny head to the Fontana complex again, to test out their new toys. They are ushered around the mansion to the back garden by one of the Italian guards. There is a target range set up on the grass that is illuminated by a set of giant floodlights.

The Don appears from the mansion, dressed as suavely as ever. He is accompanied by Mario and Bella who are also dressed to the nines, making the girls feel underdressed in jeans and a shirt.

"Are we supposed to start wearing suits twenty-four-seven now, as well?" Al whispers to her sister.

"We only have two," she replies.

"Four, if you turn them inside out."

Before Sonny has time to laugh, the family is close enough to greet. They all shake hands and kiss each other on both cheeks. The Don guides them towards the weapon table,

"Here is your pistol. This is the silencer." He holds it up to show them. "It attaches like so." He then demonstrates how to assemble it.

The girls watch intently. As soon as the silencer is attached, The Don points the gun at the target and, without looking, fires a bullet straight into the bullseye.

"Wow!" Al says in astonishment.

The Don smiles. "I did my time out in the streets."

"Clearly!" Sonny compliments.

He holds out the pistol for Sonny. "Your go."

She takes it out of his hand and steadies herself in front of the target. The tiny *ding* sound lets them know she's taken the shot, perfect bullseye again. Al has a go next, also hitting the bullseye.

"Perfect scores all round!" The Don celebrates.

He dismantles the gun and places it into a metal briefcase. He then hands the girls their new phones. "It has everybody's number in it that you will need."

"I've not had a flip-phone in years," Al says, flipping the phone open and closed with her thumb.

"Do you remember doing this?" Sonny holds the phone up to her ear like she's on a call. "'Bye!" she quips, before slapping the top of the phone down.

Al falls about laughing while the Italians look on, amused.

Bella raises an eyebrow. "These two are professional?"

"Only when we need to be." Sonny winks at her.

"Shall we go in for a drink?" The Don offers.

They agree, and head inside, where the rest of the family are chatting in the living room. The Don hides the briefcase in his office for the time being.

"Don Van de Jaager tells us you speak Dutch," Alessa says to the girls.

"A little, yeah." They smile.

"Do you speak Italian?" Mario asks.

"*Si*." Al smirks, before laughing at herself.

Mario nods contently.

"At least we have a way of communicating with you in secret now," Alessa says.

The Don nods. "It comes in handy."

An alarm sounds through the house, startling the family. The Don picks up the phone before it even rings. He says something quickly in Italian down the phone before hanging up.

"*Polizia*," he announces to the room.

The family spring into action, exiting the room to hide anything incriminating. The girls are ushered into Alessa's studio upstairs and told to hide until the coast is clear. They're left alone as the family rush around downstairs.

"Where are we supposed to hide?" Sonny asks, looking around the room.

Al shrugs and searches the room for any potential hiding places. She chooses to hide behind a rack of clothes in an open wardrobe.

"Can you see me?" she asks Sonny.

"I can see your big, flapping feet." She laughs. "Can you see me?"

Al pops her head out in between a dress and a blouse that are hanging up, to try and find her sister. It doesn't take long, as she spots Sonny's head balancing on top of a headless mannequin's body.

"Yeah."

Sonny laughs and stands in the middle of the room again, searching for another place. Suddenly, voices begin to travel up the stairs and the girls panic. Al shoves her head back behind the clothes and Sonny flusters around in the middle of the room, spinning around about twenty times, clockwise and anti-clockwise, and still no hiding place in mind.

The doors to the studio are pushed open, sending a breeze through the room.

"This is my wife's clothing studio. Maybe she can make you a suit, Detective," The Don can be heard saying.

The detective doesn't reply. He fingers through the clothes on the rack, edging closer to Al. The Don spots her feet as he searches for them himself.

"Perhaps we can speed this up. We're having some family round for dinner tonight," he urges.

"We'll stay as long as it takes," the detective states curtly, passing Al behind the rack.

She can see the top of his head over the railing, making her duck down a little bit more. She wonders where Sonny is, hoping it isn't anywhere stupid like last time.

It feels like a lifetime before the room falls quiet again. Al peeks through the clothes to see if it's safe to come out. She sees no one.

"Sonny?" she whispers loudly, stepping back into the room from her makeshift Narnia.

A pile of clothes on the floor moves and uncovers Sonny in a foetal position on the floor underneath them.

Al nods in approval of the hiding place. "Not bad."

Sonny gets up off the floor. "Last minute, you know."

"I wonder who the detective was?"

"Not sure, I was blinded by piles of fabric," Sonny says, pointing to the mountain of clothes.

The doors to the studio swing open again and the girls freeze. Sonny picks up a pair of fabric-cutting scissors from the island and holds them out in front of her, ready to attack.

Mario walks in and holds his hands up in surrender. "Please, don't hurt me."

The girls let out a sigh of relief and Sonny puts the scissors back in their place.

"Why were they here?" Al asks.

"It was a raid, but they found nothing, as usual."

"I'm not surprised. He practically looked me in the eyes and still didn't find me." Al laughs.

Mario smiles and shrugs. "They're not as smart as they come across. Apart from Leaver. He has a brain that'd be put to better use in the Mafia!"

"Have you never tried to recruit him?" Sonny asks.

He shakes his head. "He's more of a German than an Italian; he'd ruin us. Anyway, you should get home, that was a close call. We can't have any of them recognising you as Shelley's daughters."

They travel down the winding stairs to see the entire Fontana complex gathered in the hall, aunties, uncles, cousins, grandparents, the lot. All eyes are on the three of them ascending the stairs.

"*Chi sono quelli?*" An elderly woman dressed in all black asks Don Fontana to identify the two mysterious girls who are walking towards her.

He leans in closer to tell her, "*Nuovi membri della famiglia, Mama.*" (New members of the family, Mother.)

She nods open-mouthed, still looking at the girls.

"*Ciao, Nonna,*" Mario greets his grandmother, kissing both her cheeks.

"Oh, ciao, Luca." She smiles, patting him on the cheek.

He quickly glances at The Don. *"Sono Mario, Nonna."* (I'm Mario, Nana.)

"Mario," she repeats, obliviously.

"Questi sono Al e Sonny." The Don introduces her to the girls.

She takes their hands in hers. *"Siete belle e intelligente."* (You're beautiful and intelligent.)

"Grazie..." The girls search for a name.

"Nonna," Mario supplies, with a smile.

The girls kiss her on the cheek. *"Grazie, Nonna."*

Some more family members come over to introduce themselves, but others are not interested. Sonny wonders how she's ever going to remember that many names, especially since they're all so similar. They wish everyone goodnight and The Don distributes the metal briefcase to them at the door, out of sight of any unknowing family members.

"Buona fortuna." He wishes them good luck before closing the door.

CHAPTER NINE

The next morning, the girls lie to their parents about where they're going for the day; this information will come back to their dad, and they wouldn't want to be linked to the scene of the crime. They gather their camping equipment, tent, blow-up beds, silenced pistol and snacks. They also shove a couple of old wigs on their heads, and Sonny finds a pair of old glasses to wear- hoping it's enough for them to not be recognised.

Sonny decides to drive them there. On the way, they listen to their throwback playlist from the late '90s and early 2000s and sing along like they used to do with their mum and cousins when they were younger, on their regular road trip to Abersoch.

The journey is flawless and they make it to the

island in time, before the afternoon tide rolls in and blockades the bridge to the island.

"Do we know where he's pitched up?" Sonny asks, as they walk towards the check-in counter.

"No, but this is how we find out."

They step up to the counter and Al hands over the ticket she booked online.

"What's your postcode?" the geeky man behind the counter asks.

"WA3 8TS," Al lies, instead using the postcode of Detective Leaver.

He types it into the computer. "Ah, we've already had this postcode on here. Are you Stella and Julie Pinborough?"

"That's us! We're meeting up with our neighbours, the Leaver family. Could you tell us where they're pitched up? We haven't been able to get hold of them," Al tells him.

He starts tapping away at the computer again. "I can certainly have a look, but they may have moved."

"Great," Sonny says, smiling and looking around the small lobby.

"They should be in section three, here's a map to help you." He beams as he hands it to them.

"Thank you! Have a nice day," they say sweetly, before heading back to the car.

Al directs Sonny through the sand dunes as best as she can, but soon the road turns to sand and it's hard to gather her bearings.

Al points straight ahead. "There he is!"

Sonny steps on it and speeds towards Detective Leaver and his family.

"I thought we were gonna shoot him, not fucking run them all over," Al says.

"Trust," she says quickly, too busy concentrating on her driving.

Right in front of Leavers' tent, Sonny turns the steering wheel and the car spins sideways, digging the tyres into the sand. They're stuck. Sonny revs the engine but the tyres don't budge.

She rolls her window down. "Little help?" She laughs innocently.

Detective Leaver comes to the rescue. He digs out some of the sand around the tyres and pushes the car from behind, and eventually the treads grip onto the sand and the car crawls back onto solid ground. She parks up and they both climb out of the car.

"Thank you so much for helping! This is our first camping trip on our own so we're a bit clueless," Sonny explains, trying to seem as young and innocent as possible.

His hard-looking face softens into a sort of smile. "We're all seasoned campers, we can help you." He beckons to his family, who are sitting around a disposable barbecue. "We're only here for one more night, though."

"Oh, don't worry about it, I'm sure that's all we'll need." Al smiles at him.

"Yeah, we're only here for tonight, anyway," Sonny adds.

He squints the sun out of his eyes and nods. "Do you need any help putting up your tent?"

Sonny pulls it out of the boot of her car. "No, it's okay, we have a pop-up! We might need help putting it back down, though."

"No problem," he says, and waves to them as he goes back to join his family.

Sonny drags the tent out of its casing and it pops open, spilling out onto the grass, forming a perfect pyramid shape.

"That was easy." Sonny smiles at Al.

They bash the pegs into the ground so the tent won't fly away, and fill it with their blow-up beds and sleeping bags. They crawl inside and decide to play it cool; they'll wait for Leaver to talk to them first.

"So, how are we going to do this?" Sonny asks quietly.

Al shoves a handful of crisps into her mouth. "Easily."

"Yeah, but you haven't actually told me the plan."

She swallows the mouthful of potato and wipes her mouth. "So, I was thinking, I'll distract the family, we'll go on a walk or something. As he's helping you pack away the tent, shoot him and roll him up in it."

Sonny nods in approval of the plan.

"If we time it right, the tide will be coming in just as we reach the bridge. That's when we push his body into the ocean and, hopefully, he'll never be seen again."

"Wow!" Sonny says, shaking her head. "You're an evil genius."

Al shrugs, with a smile. "What can I say?"

As if on cue, a shadowy figure appears outside the tent. "Hey, girls. Do you have anything to eat for dinner?" the voice says, fingers tapping on the door of the tent a couple of times.

Sonny unzips it. "Oh, hello again. Erm... We don't."

"You can join us, if you like? We have burgers and sausages," Detective Leaver invites them.

The girls smile brightly. "That sounds great, thank you!"

They grab their lounge chairs and join the Leaver family around the fire.

"This is my wife, Cassie, and my two children, Tom and Claire," he introduces, "and I'm Ed."

"Nice to meet you all," the girls say.

"I'm S–" Sonny begins to tell them.

Al interrupts to stop her from revealing their real names. "I'm Julie, and this is my twin sister, Stella."

Detective Leaver tries not to laugh. "Stella... That's an unusual name."

"Yeah, our parents didn't love me, clearly." Sonny throws an unamused look to Al, who shrugs back at her.

"Where are your parents? Are they not the camping type?" Cassie asks them politely.

"They're dead."

Al looks from Sonny to the Leaver family and nods with an exaggerated sad face.

"Aww, you poor girls," Cassie says, nearly crying.

"How did they die?" Leaver asks.

Cassie hits him on the arm. "Don't ask that!"

"No, no, it's okay. It was a long time ago now." Al reassures them. "We were at the zoo and they both fell into an enclosure, they got ripped apart," she explains, with a big, sad sigh.

"What enclosure?" their little boy, Tom, asks.

"The meerkats," Al says quickly, pulling yet another sad face and nodding slowly.

The family look at each other, not sure if they're joking or not. They all wait for the other to say something. It's Sonny that breaks the silence,

"She's joking... It was the gorillas."

"Aw, that's such an unbelievable tragedy." Cassie recoils at the thought of it.

"Unbelievable, yes, but inevitable." Sonny continues to add to the surreal story.

"Anyway, enough about us. Tell us about your family," Al diverts, not wanting the story to become any more ridiculous.

Leaver begins to distribute the burgers onto plates. "I'm a Detective Constable, my wife is a vet. We've been married for fifteen years now," Leaver explains. "And these two rascals were born ten years ago." He points to them with his spatula.

The little girl jumps out of her seat. "We're twins!"

Al gasps dramatically. "No way! I wish I was a twin." She lies, again, hoping to throw Leaver off the scent of who they really are; he would know Shelley has two twin girls.

"We do everything together," Tom adds, jumping up like his sister.

"What do you like doing?" Sonny asks them.

They both start reeling off activities over the top of each other, but 'swimming' managed to be heard over the loud muddle of words.

"We can go swimming after we've eaten, if you like?" Sonny suggests.

"Yeah!" the kids scream, jumping around.

They wolf down their food and chat a little bit more, before Cassie accompanies them to the sea to watch over them. They play volleyball and have swimming races all day, the cold Welsh waters relieving them from the scorching sun.

"There's going to be a storm tomorrow," Cassie tells the girls, as they return to dry land.

Al wraps a towel around herself. "I believe so. Everybody will probably be leaving tomorrow."

"Probably. We had the whole week booked, but there's no point in staying in that sort of weather. It's just dangerous," Cassie explains.

Sonny catches up with them, the children in tow behind her. "Very dangerous indeed."

That night, after the children have gone to bed, the girls stay up drinking with Cassie and Detective Leaver. The early signs of a storm begin to approach; thick, dark clouds and rumbling thunder float by above their heads.

"Have you ever been to Swaziland?" Leaver asks the girls, after telling them a story about him being there.

"Yeah, we loved it!" they lie. They've barely even heard of it.

"Whereabouts did you stay?" Cassie asks.

Sonny looks to Al for an answer. Al racks her brain, trying to conjure up a place name. "Erm... The capital..."

Leaver's eyes narrow. "What is the capital again?"

"You tell us, you're the one that loves it so much, ha-ha." Sonny tries to deflect the inquisition.

"I want to test your knowledge."

Al closes her eyes and tries to picture the flags of the world book from when they were kids. She can see the pages flicking through her memory until she gets to 'S' – the flag stands boldly on the left-hand side, the capital city and other information noted below.

"Mbabane," she says confidently, getting ready to tell him what the population was in 1999.

He nods. "Correct. I've only been Mbabane once. Where did you stay?"

"Not sure, it was ages ago now," Al says, getting frustrated at the constant questions.

"We try to go to Africa at least once a year, don't we, honey?" he says, taking hold of Cassie's hand.

"We do." She beams. "We're constantly on holiday!" She laughs obnoxiously.

The girls roll their eyes secretly. "Whoa!"

"How do you get all the time off work?" Sonny questions.

He takes a swig from his beer. "I do what I want. I practically run the show." He shrugs.

"We know someone who works there, too," Al admits, wanting him to say something wrong, giving her more of an excuse to kill him.

"Who is it?"

"Tim Shelley." She says the name passively, like there's no real connection.

He snorts. "How do you know that loser?"

The girls look at each other sternly and then back to Leaver.

"He was our dad's friend," Sonny tells him.

"Then your dad had a poor choice in judgement." He points at them with his beer can.

Cassie gasps. "Edward! You can't say that!" she spits, before turning to a whisper. "He's dead."

Leaver grumbles.

Al says, "We should get to bed. We've got a big

day tomorrow, haven't we?" She stands and picks up her folding chair.

"Thanks for your hospitality. Are you still okay to put our tent down for us?" Sonny asks.

"Of course. Goodnight, girls," he mumbles, partly from embarrassment.

They fold away their chairs and crawl into the tent. They get into their sleeping bags fully clothed and turn the dim lantern off. The wind begins to pick up and the tent rustles constantly; this, as well as the harrowing whistle that sings Detective Leaver his last lullaby, makes it impossible to switch off.

"Shall we have a one pot?" Sonny asks through the darkness.

"Go on then."

Sonny grabs the bag full of their weed paraphernalia and begins to roll a small spliff. "God, I can't wait to kill him. 'We try to go to Africa at least once a year.' What a dickhead!"

"We're always on holiday aren't we, sweetie darling?" Al mocks them in a snobby accent.

They laugh dirtily for a moment until the spliff is ready to be smoked.

Sonny takes a long drag. "Aah, that's nice," she says, as the smoke billows out of her mouth.

"I wonder what Dad's gonna think about this?"

"He'll probably be relieved," Sonny replies, passing Al the spliff.

Al takes a drag. "I hope so."

As soon as the spliff is done, they throw it out of the tent through a tiny flap and fall straight to sleep.

The next morning, they are awoken early by a blistering storm. The tent is practically flat from the continual pressure of the wind and the girls find that they can barely think over the racket of the hammering rain. They unzip the tent door to see the Leaver family already packing away their tent and equipment.

"Shit, we've got to get moving," Sonny says, nudging her sister.

Al checks her watch. "Don't worry, we've got twenty minutes."

They get ready regardless, making it more like fifteen minutes. Sonny constructs the pistol and silencer before hiding it in her waistband.

"Ready?" Al asks.

Sonny nods assertively.

They wander out of the tent, wrapped up in their waterproof coats, and approach the family.

"Good morning!" they shout through the storm.

"Nothing good about it!" Detective Leaver replies, scowling.

Sonny goes over to help him with the tent pegs and to keep the tent on the floor, rather than it being carried away into the sky. Al stands with Cassie and the two young children.

"How long is your drive back?" she asks Cassie.

"Oh, about three hours, I think!" she answers, looking fed up.

Al puts on a look of theatrically exaggerated shock. "Maybe we should go to the toilet now before we set off."

"Good idea. Do you need the toilet?" Cassie asks her children.

"Yeah!" they scream.

"Honey, we're going to go to the toilet before we leave!" Cassie shouts over to her husband.

He gives them a quick thumbs-up, having more on his mind than his family's toilet habits.

Sonny gives them a kind smile and a wave as they begin their five-minute walk to the closest toilet stalls. Once the Leavers' giant tent is packed away, Sonny asks again if he'll help put their tent down, too, which, of course, he agrees to. She has a quick look round; there are no other tents in the vicinity anymore.

They take the pegs out and Leaver jumps on top of the tent to flatten it down. Sonny takes this time to pull the gun out of her waistband.

She takes a second to line up the shot before she shoots him at point blank range in the back, the bullet travelling straight to his heart. He dies instantly and Sonny rolls him up in the tent and keeps him securely in there by attaching the tent clips, before too much blood spills out onto the field. She drags him towards her car and, after a lot of huffing, manages to shove him across the back seat. She gets into the driver's side and starts the engine.

Once Al and the Leaver family make it to the toilets, they all shut themselves into their individual stalls. Al quietly takes off her shoes and leaves them in front of the toilet. She slowly pries open the stall door and locks it behind her, using a coin. This way, the family will be waiting for her for as long as possible, believing she's still in the stall. She tiptoes out of the door, where Sonny pulls up outside. She rushes into the passenger's seat and looks behind her, seeing the wrapped-up body lying in the back.

"Let's go," Al says, letting out a big sigh of relief and adrenaline.

They get to the bridge, which is already swelling with water. Al gets out and wades through the shin-deep water in her socks, towards the back doors. She drags Leaver out by his feet and his body splashes onto the ground. She pushes him through the bridge's railing and she can feel his body fall out of her hands and begin to sink. She quickly dives back into the car and they speed off the bridge, making their way back home in time for lunch.

Cassie and her children stand shivering in the small building that homes the toilets. "She's been in there for an awfully long time," Cassie observes.

Claire kneels on the floor, looking under the stall door. "She has no feet."

"What? Don't be absurd!" Cassie shouts.

"No, really. There are no legs in the shoes, look!" Claire orders her mother to kneel, too.

She pulls an irritated face before swooping her head below the door, where she sees only an empty pair of shoes in front of the toilet. She frowns. "Let's go back to your dad," she suggests, taking tight hold of her children's hands.

When they get back to the site, however, there is nobody there. Just the family car and a pile of camping equipment that is now soaked with rain.

Al peels her sopping wet socks off her feet and wrings them dry out of the car window.

"Where are your shoes?" Sonny laughs, only just realising Al's barefoot.

"Well, they weren't actually my shoes, but I left them in the toilet."

"Literally *in* the toilet?"

Al sniggers. "Nah, in front of the toilet, like someone's sat there."

"That's so tight. Bet they're still waiting there now!"

"I hope he didn't have their car keys in his pocket or something." Al cringes.

Sonny winces, too. "Probs should have checked that before he sunk to the bottom of the ocean."

Detective Leaver did in fact have the car keys in his pocket. Cassie and the two children investigate the entire island, but nobody's seen him. They call the police but, due to the high tide, they can't get to the island until tomorrow morning, when, by that time, all the evidence will have vanished. Even the pool of blood on the field has now been swallowed by the soil and the rain. The girls have pulled off their first meticulous murder for the Fontana family.

CHAPTER TEN

B efore heading inside, Al slips on a pair of trainers from her bag – trainers that are actually hers this time. When they get indoors, only Karen is home, clashing pots and pans in the kitchen. The girls run upstairs and hide anything incriminating until they can give them back to the Fontanas tonight. They casually stroll back down the stairs and go into the kitchen to talk to their mother.

"We're *baaack!*" Sonny shouts.

Karen jumps and spins around with wide eyes. "God! Don't do that." She calms down and gives them a hug and a poke in the ribs for laughing. "How was your trip?"

"Fine."

"No troubles?" Karen raises an eyebrow.

"None," they both say innocently.

Karen goes back to sifting through the drawer of pans.

"Is Dad at work?" Sonny asks.

"Yeah, he said he'll be back late. Something's gone on," Karen explains, without even glancing away from the drawer.

Al and Sonny look at each other but not in worry; they know they'll never be caught. They tell Karen that they're going out, to which she replies, "You two are never home!"

They reply with some passive comment, then grab the metal briefcase and hide it in the car, ready for later, and head out into town. They decide to eat in a small Italian café that always smells deliciously of garlic. They order some antipasti to share together, rather than a full meal, and they both order an Italian beer, to celebrate.

"Cheers!" Sonny holds the pint glass across the table.

"Tits, ass, ass, tits!" they say, hitting the top of the glasses together, then the bottom twice, and back to the top again.

They both take a big gulp of beer and let out a thirsty gasp afterwards. "Needed that," Sonny says, looking at the glass.

Silence falls between them for a moment, as they are unsure of what to say to each other.

"Do you feel any different?" Al mumbles.

Sonny thinks about it for a minute. "Not really."

"How? I didn't even do it and I already feel even eviller than before."

"We were going to hell anyway." Sonny laughs.

Al tries not to laugh, so as to not admit it, but she smirks and nods slightly.

The waiter brings over their dishes and they thank him,

"We have a wonderful singer coming on in a minute," he tells them.

"Oh, really? Who is it?" Al asks, with a smile.

"Hannah," is all he gives them before telling them to enjoy their meal, then he retreats back to the kitchen.

The measly crowd of customers begin to applaud as a young woman, wearing what is clearly a blonde wig, steps up onto the small stage.

"Here she is, our Hannah," Sonny scoffs, with a mouthful of cheesy garlic bread.

"Good old H."

The woman sits solemnly on a stool, waiting for the music to kick in. The crowd waits in anticipation. The old guy trying to work the audio can be seen fiddling with wires and buttons but nothing seems to be working.

Without even lifting her head, Hannah screams, "COME ON!"

Al and Sonny look at each other with shocked expressions, trying to stifle their laughter.

Finally, after a younger staff member comes to

help, the music begins to play. A dainty piano number. Hannah's voice is not bad at all, but there are some notes that she just cannot hit, and every time she misses one, the girls pull a cringing face at each other.

On the second song, Sonny squints hard and then quickly turns back to her sister.

"It's Zeta!" she reveals.

Al frowns. "Who?"

"Zeta Fontana!" Sonny laughs.

Al tries to focus in on the singer's face but can't quite make it out, so she just shrugs it off. They continue eating, until Al nearly chokes on her risotto. Al hunches forward with her hand over her mouth, Sonny can see her shoulders jittering up and down, which automatically makes her laugh, too,

"What?" Sonny asks, between wheezes.

Al looks up. Her eyes are streaming, her face is red and she can hardly breathe. She swallows a big mouthful of beer and calms down before explaining, "I've just thought about what her name must be – Hannah Fontana!" She just manages to get the name out before starting to giggle again.

Sonny bursts out laughing. "She's got the best of both worlds."

They start cackling now, drawing attention from the crowd and Hannah Fontana herself. Zeta recognises them immediately; she thinks they're laughing at her singing and so she storms off the stage in an embarrassed rage, giving the girls daggers as she leaves.

"That's defo Zeta then, seen that look before," Al says.

Sonny nods, wide-eyed in agreement. They finish their food and down the rest of their pints before trying to find Zeta. She is in the side alley smoking a cigarette when the girls step outside of the café.

"Alright, Zeta?" they ask her, lighting their own cigs now.

"*Vaffanculo!*" she spits viciously. (Fuck off.)

"Rude," Sonny says, pulling a disappointed face.

"I'll tell you what is rude," she begins, walking closer to the girls now. "Laughing at my singing in front of everybody!"

Al shifts on her feet. "There were only about three people in there."

"Two of them were us," Sonny adds.

"And the third one was you." Al nods towards Zeta and Sonny starts sniggering again.

Zeta swings for Sonny, but before her fist can get anywhere, Sonny has her pinned up against the wall, her forearm across Zeta's neck. "We're part of the same family now, Zeta. Don't make me kill you," Sonny says quietly.

Zeta screams, trying with all her might to break free. Al leans against the opposite wall, smoking, unastonished by the commotion. A stranger walks past the side alley and stops when he sees what's happening. Al gives him a smile and a thumbs-up, prompting him to rush back to his daily activities, leaving them alone again.

Zeta gives up the struggle. "Okay! Just let me go."

Sonny steps back and Zeta rubs her neck. "You're crazy," she tells Sonny.

"Yup."

"We weren't laughing at your singing, by the way," Al tells her.

Zeta's expression softens. "Oh..."

"We were laughing at your name." Sonny ruins the mood.

Zeta goes off on a rage again, swinging at Sonny for a second time. Al grabs her hand in the air, and Sonny takes the opportunity to lay a punch to Zeta's stomach. She folds over in pain and slumps to the floor.

Sonny turns to Al. "I didn't even do it that hard."

Al rolls her eyes and shakes her head as if to say, 'I know, what a wimp.' She crouches down to level herself with Zeta.

"If you try to hit my sister again, I'll kill you myself," Al threatens.

Zeta looks up at her. Her mouth is open but there is no sound coming out.

"Can we be friends now?"

Zeta nods, stunned.

"Great," Al says, smiling now.

Sonny helps her pick Zeta up off the floor.

"There you go, mate," Sonny says, wiping invisible debris off Zeta's shoulder.

She still cannot reply.

The girls look at each other in amusement.

"Anyway, we're off now," says Sonny.

"Have a nice day, try not to get into any trouble," Al adds, as they walk out of the alleyway.

Zeta remains stationary, apart from her hands slowly moving to her bruised stomach. The old man who owns the building finds her outside and ushers her back into the café for a coffee. She tells him she'll be taking a break from singing for a while.

At work, Detective Shelley and his squad are working on the whereabouts of their colleague. They were alerted by the Welsh police this morning, after Detective Leaver was reported missing from the island. They check his phone records for anything out of the ordinary. Shelley spots a call made from Leaver's mobile to a landline in Manchester that he recognises as belonging to the Fontanas.

He tells the room about his revolutionary find. "This must have something to do with them," he reckons.

"Leaver was hounding them. He was the one who ordered that raid the other day. Maybe they're getting him back," another detective explains.

Shelley leans back on his chair. "We have no evidence, and nobody can get onto the island until tomorrow."

"Sounds like the Fontanas. Conniving bastards," another detective says scornfully. "We should just go and eliminate them all."

Shelley frowns in disbelief. "We can't do that. We need to find sufficient evidence to arrest them. A lifetime in prison is more justice than being killed. Besides, eyewitness accounts point towards two female suspects, apparently named Julie and Stella, none of which appear in the Fontana family tree."

"Oh, fuck off, Shelley. This mess is all your fault, anyway."

"Tell me how?" Shelley confronts his colleague.

The other detective gets out of his chair. "By arresting Holdis. If you hadn't gone against what everyone else told you to do, then the Italians wouldn't have this much power!"

"But the Germans would have it, and they'd kill you all in an instant if you gave them the opportunity!" Shelley raises his voice, too.

"Go 'ome, Shelleh. This type of discussion in't for people like you," the Commissioner says, leaning unnoticed in the doorway.

Everyone turns to look at him. He has a Caesar mod haircut and an aggressive resting face, and he walks around like he's ready to head-butt anyone, at any minute. The other detectives calm down, knowing Shelley doesn't have a leg to stand on against the Commissioner.

Shelley stays seated, trying to think of something to say. He doesn't want to get fired, but he also doesn't want whatever plans they conjure up to go ahead. Then he realises they'll happen with or without him being present. He grits his teeth and stands up, collecting his coat and car keys. Everybody watches him silently leave the room.

Together, the detectives decide to ambush the Fontana complex tonight, full SWAT team and all – which was, of course, vetoed by the Commissioner.

That night, the girls drive through the complex and everything is back to normal. The families are in their own houses, full of light and warmth, just as it should be. They are wearing their latest suits gifted by the Fontanas; that, along with 50 Cent's *In Da Club* blasting through the speakers and a pistol in the back, makes them feel like the ultimate modern-day gangsters. There are a few armed bodyguards patrolling the complex because of the latest raid, their fingers are always sitting on their gun's trigger.

Sonny parks the car outside the front door of Don Fontana's mansion whilst Al retrieves the briefcase from under the seat, and together they walk up to the door and ring the bell. Don Fontana answers and greets them both with a double kiss and handshake combo that is favoured by every European, and he invites them inside.

"How did the mission go?" he asks them, as they make their way to his office.

"It went very smoothly," Al tells him. "Sonny did a great job."

Sonny simulates a bashful acceptance of the compliment. "Couldn't have done it without you."

The Don opens the office door for the girls and as they enter, they're greeted by the full Fontana gang, Mario, Luca, Lorenzo and a couple of gruff-looking button men. They're all smoking cigars and drinking whisky.

When the girls walk in, all eyes are on them. Mario and Luca rise first, greeting them both with kisses and handshakes again. Al feels like Christmas came early, having all these handsome Italians leaving their mark on her cheeks. Sonny wishes the genders were swapped, but is happy nonetheless. Lorenzo offers a formal handshake, shortly followed by the same from the two button men.

"You won't have met my two friends here. This is Antonio." The Don gestures to the smaller man, who's now sat back down on the soft leather couch.

He's around five foot tall, and probably has the same circumference. He has dirty olive skin with dark, dusty rings under his small, all-seeing eyes. His black hair shows signs of thinning towards the crown, but the rest is thick and covered in gel.

The Don then motions to the other button man sitting next to Antonio. "And this is Stefano."

Stefano smirks and nods towards them. He is a tall, well-built man with light brown shoulder-length hair and an extremely neat walrus moustache. His face is kind and doesn't have a single blemish in sight. Although, he does look like his moustache is always tickling his nose by the way his face creases every now and again.

Mario fixes them both a drink and the girls settle wherever there is a seat. Sonny manages to bag the only single couch left, meaning Al, the smallest in the room, is left sitting in the miniscule gap in between the two biggest, Mario and Stefano. It is comical to see and even think that she will be the mastermind behind killings that these two men will soon be undertaking.

"So, tell us how you did it," Luca pushes eagerly.

All eyes are on Al.

"Well... It was simple, really. I used my dad's work computer to see where Leaver was and I found an e-mail that said he was on the Island with his family all week, so that's where I started from," she explains, having to strain her neck to make eye contact with either Mario or Stefano.

"I checked the tide times. There are some days where there is only one timeframe for the bridge being open, so I thought we would do it the day before this interval. Erm... yeah, so we went and got speaking to the family and then there was that big storm so everyone was packing away. I stalled the rest of the family by making us all walk the five minutes to the closest toilet. That's when Sonny did her business." Al points to Sonny to continue that part of the story.

Sonny swallows her mouthful of wine and takes over the narrative. "Yeah, he just jumped on top of our tent. I shot him in the back so the bullet would travel through to his heart, which it did. He died instantly so I just rolled him up in the tent, secured it, put him in the car and then we drove to the bridge."

"How did you get rid of the body?" Stefano asks, in a very deep, husky Italian accent.

Al smiles, knowing this was the best part of her plan. "Well, I'll tell you, Stefano! We timed it so that, by the time we made it to the bridge, we had literal seconds until it disappeared underwater. I got out and just pushed the tent through the railings and I felt him slip away under the current."

They all nod in approval.

"So, all round success then." Luca smiles. "You're a natural."

Al laughs. "I don't know about that."

Suddenly, the sound of gunfire echoes through the complex and everyone is on high alert. The Don frowns and hurriedly picks up the phone.

There is no word from security. He slams the phone back onto the receiver and swears in Italian.

"Wait here," he says to everyone, but motions for Antonio, Stefano and Lorenzo to follow him.

Mario stands to exit with them.

"No! You stay, look after the rest," The Don insists.

He obeys his father, but still heads over to the secret weapon stash behind the bookcase. He takes out an MG4 and sets it up on his father's desk.

"Luca, I know you've never killed anyone, but prepare to do so now. Our lives depend on it. Something is clearly not right," Mario orders him.

Luca sits behind the gun that is facing the door,

"If anyone comes in, shoot them all."

Luca gulps and nods vigorously.

Mario then passes the girls their own pistols along with a couple of extra ammo clips. He then equips himself with a huge AK-47.

"Why don't we get one of them?" Sonny questions.

"Do you know how to use one?" Mario asks.

"No..." she replies.

He offers no response apart from a 'that's why' shrug.

Gunshots are constant now. It's only when screaming can be heard that Mario can't hide any longer. He rushes towards the door,

"Right. Stay here. I'll come back once I find out what's going on. Look after yourselves."

The door shuts behind him and Al, Sonny and Luca are left alone in the room, still blissfully unaware of what real danger lurks beyond the walls. Luca shots the rest of his whisky and shivers as it travels down to his stomach. The girls have their pistols at their sides, ready to use them.

After what seems like an eternity, the office door swings open and Mario and Antonio burst in. They all seem extremely worn out.

"Where's the rest?" Luca shouts, pushing himself out of the chair.

Mario slams the door closed again. "Don't worry. Dad is in the saferoom and Lorenzo drove the girls to the safehouse."

"What about Stefano?" Luca asks again.

"I don't know." Mario runs his hand through his now limp hair.

"What's actually going on then?" Al asks impatiently.

"We're being ambushed by a SWAT team. They're taking no prisoners. A few of the security guards have already been found dead," Antonio explains.

They all take a moment to let the severity of the situation sink in.

"So, it's kill or be killed?" Sonny hypothesises.

Mario nods glumly, biting his lip.

"They'll be making their way here for The Don, so be ready," Antonio orders, on his way to exit the room.

"Luca, you stay here. You two," Mario turns to Al and Sonny, "just... look after yourselves the best you can." His sad eyes linger on Al.

"We'll be fine. We can do it," Sonny assures him.

They all exit the room one after another and split up, leaving Luca alone with his thoughts and a powerful machine gun.

Al and Sonny decide to take refuge upstairs, where there are numerous podiums surrounding the landing that they could hide behind. It would also give them the uphill advantage on any targets filing through the entrance hall.

An enormous boom rattles the mansion. They're breaking down the door. Another boom, this time accompanied by the crack of the wood giving in slightly.

Al takes a deep, steadying breath and locks eyes with Sonny, on the other side of the open, square landing. They nod 'good luck' to each other with fearful eyes but steady hands, their fingers ready on the trigger.

The double doors shatter onto the marble flooring and a smoke bomb clatters across the hall and deploys just below the stairs. As the room fills with smoke, thin, shimmering green lasers search the room.

"Shit," both of the girls whisper to themselves without realising.

Nobody wants to be the first to shoot. The girls continue to survey the armed intruders from the safe haven of the landing. One of the SWAT team shoots down the corridor at nothing in particular, setting off a prolonged burst of gunfire. Now is their time. The girls unleash a shower of bullets down onto the enemy and soon enough, those green lasers are frantically trying to locate any kind of movement.

Because of the smoke, the girls are essentially guessing where their targets are, but thanks to the lasers, they're mostly accurate guesses. Sonny thinks how satisfying it is to see those green lasers drop to the floor one by one, until there are none left. The smoke finally clears and they look at each other across the landing again. They smile this time, out of relief. But it is short-lived, as a deadlier second wave appears.

Their guns are held tightly to their body as they step over the corpses of their comrades. Al can't help but have a peek around the pillar to see how many there are. One of the SWAT team spots her, and a bullet narrowly misses her face, instead indenting the intricate, white stone column. She ducks back behind it to regain her cool, while Sonny barrages them with bullets once again.

Al steadies her heartbeat and runs to the next column, shooting as she goes. The *ping* of close-by bullets is terrifying, but fuels the girls with an extra dose of much needed adrenaline.

The SWAT team begin slowly scaling the stairs in formation, their guns swinging from side to side trying to cover all potential vantage points. But it isn't enough; most of the soldiers are shot dead on the way up. Their rigid bodies, covered in heavy armour, slump down the stairs headfirst like useless, tangled Slinkies.

Sonny reloads using her last ammo clip; she desperately needs to finish them all off with this remaining round of bullets. Within seconds, she guns down over half of the squad with deadly precision. The last two surviving enemies make it to the top of the split staircase, one heading either side towards the girls.

They take refuge behind the final pair of columns on the landing, the only ones not riddled with bullet holes.

"How much ammo do you have?" Sonny asks her sister quietly.

"Not a lot," Al replies worriedly.

Sonny exhales heavily. "How long do we have?" she asks, referring to how much time until they're shot by their impending assailants.

Al thinks carefully before she answers. "Five seconds."

Sonny nods defiantly, "Now."

They both quickly drop to their knees and peer

around the pillar, their pistols out in front of them. Al squeezes the trigger and the bullet pierces a hole right in between her target's eyes and he slowly slumps to the floor in phases. The legs are the first to go, then the arms, and finally, he falls flat on his face and a crimson river pools out of him and is absorbed into the cream carpet, just like syrup trickling into a snow cone.

Sonny pulls the trigger, and the dreaded click of an empty barrel seals her fate. She takes a quick glance from her target to the pistol, and back to look into his eyes. He smirks at her. Her muscles loosen and her blood drains as she comes to terms with death. With a deep breath, she closes her eyes and a deafening shot echoes against the high ceilings.

She peels her eyelid open to see the SWAT member dead on the floor, his blood quickly pooling and dripping off the landing, down onto the marble floor in the hall. She looks to her right. Al's gun is still poking between the banister rails. Even from across the room, Sonny can see it shaking violently. They both fall onto their backs, breathing heavily with relief and lingering fear.

"Sonny?" Al calls to her sister.

"Yeah?"

"Look at this."

Sonny turns her head to look. Al holds her pistol up towards the ceiling and shoots – that same empty click can be heard.

"Shit, that was lucky," Sonny gasps.

Al silently nods to herself, open-mouthed, unable to do anything.

"We need another gun!" Sonny remembers it isn't over yet.

They both throw themselves down the stairs and into the office. Luca grabs hold of the gun, far too late; the girls had already made it to the secret weapon stash before he even had the chance to crawl out from under the desk.

"Oh, I'm so glad you're alive!" he shouts.

"Don't speak too soon," Sonny says. She reloads the pistol as well as picking up another, more menacing-looking hand gun.

"It's crazy out there," Luca states, edging closer to the window.

He looks up at the thundering helicopters overheard. "There's helicopters…"

"Get away from the window!" Sonny shouts.

As she says this, the glass smashes into a thousand pieces as a shower of bullets is unleashed from the helicopter. Luca ducks back under the safety of the desk. The girls look at each other, anxious about Luca's safety.

Al clips more ammo into her trusty pistol. "Let's go."

The two girls head out of the room as Luca looks on from in between the slit in the desk. Al goes first and is met with the terrifying scene of heavily armed men closing in on the office.

"Shit!" she screams, diving into the opposite room.

Bullets fly down the corridor and Sonny partly closes the office door so she can watch without having to be completely exposed to the bombardment. One of the enemies throws tear gas into the room that Al has taken refuge in.

"I'm gonna step back and open the doors. Just shoot!" Sonny orders Luca, who is shaking. Only his eyes can be seen behind the desk.

He takes his seat behind the gun and Sonny flings the doors open. Luca holds onto the trigger, the row of bullets disappearing into the chamber. Once they're all gone, Sonny dives into the hallway, shooting the last remaining targets, before ducking back into the office to shield her eyes from the burning smoke bellowing from the room opposite.

"IT'S CLEAR, AL!" she screams.

Al emerges from the smoke, holding her bloodied eyes. "Sonny, I can't see!" she cries.

Al holds her hand out for any saviour, trying to find her way at the same time. Sonny grabs hold of her and, along with Luca, they all climb out of the office window into the fresh night-time air.

"We need to get some cold water into her eyes," Luca says anxiously, looking around.

"I'll go. You stay here with her." Sonny gives him

her pistol and she ventures back into the house through the broken front door.

She rushes to the kitchen and grabs a couple of bottles out of the fridge. She dashes out of the kitchen door and runs straight into Mario. They both jump and point their guns at each other until they realise who they're aiming at. Mario's face is flushed and wet with tears.

"What's wrong?" Sonny asks him.

"They got Calvino," he sobs.

Sonny wishes she could stop and console him but she has her own sibling to save.

"I'm so sorry, Mario, but Al needs me," she explains, heading back down the corridor.

"What's happened to her?" he asks, snapping out of his own mourning.

"Tear gas," she shouts over her shoulder.

Mario follows her outside to see Al still lying on the floor, white liquid pouring down her face from her eyes. Luca has hold of her hand and is using his other to stroke her hair.

Sonny kneels beside her and holds her head up to pour the cold water over her eyes.

Some of the surrounding land is on fire, including Nonna Fontana's house. Mario's sadness turns to rage and he storms off, looking for someone to take his anger out on, but every single SWAT team member is now dead. The only target left is the helicopter.

Mario climbs into the office via the window and

arms himself with a ginormous missile launcher. He props it against the empty window frame and lines up his target. The missile ejects with a satisfying pop and they all watch it travel towards the helicopter, almost as if they're expecting fireworks to explode instead of the helicopter and the people inside along with it.

The scariest part is seeing the mechanical fireball dwindle closer and closer to the complex. It crashes into the fountain in the middle of the roundabout that separates off towards various houses, spraying water and debris for miles across the complex. As they lie on the grass, observing the catastrophic bombsite, the group of young mobsters allow their adrenaline to diminish as they realise the fight is finally over.

The Don sits in the saferoom, watching the surveillance footage. He leans back in his chair and holds his face in his hands. Nobody should have to watch their son die through a television screen, like it's some kind of spectacle, but he knows he is too old and slow to have been any use in the defensive attack. He doesn't yet know the extent of his losses, but all will become clear tomorrow, once all the smoke and fire has subsided and the clear-up begins.

CHAPTER ELEVEN

W hen The Don is given the all-clear to come out, he sets about making sure everybody gets the treatment they need. The family doctor is called to the complex and a makeshift hospital is set up in The Don's mansion.

Al, Stefano, a dozen guards and Calvino are all lined up on massage beds in a cleared-out room. The doctor administers some drops into Al's swollen eyes, telling her that her vision should start to improve within a few minutes.

Stefano has been shot in the leg and the bullet has lodged in his flesh. The doctor uses his surgical tweezers to remove the bullet before disinfecting and stitching up the hole. He will make a quick and full recovery.

However, there is nothing he can do about

Calvino. He had jumped in front of a bullet for his mother as they were all escaping the complex. It killed him instantly.

As Al's vision begins to come back, the dim lights blind her still.

"Al, are you okay?" Sonny asks her.

She looks around hopelessly to find her. "Yeah, I'm still a bit blind, though. Where are you?"

"I'm here." She takes hold of Al's hand. "We're gonna have to go home soon, it's four in the morning."

"Really?" She squints in astonishment.

"Really. Let me know when you feel ready."

"We can go now. Just guide me."

She slides off the massage bed and Sonny grabs onto Al's arm. As they walk past the other beds, Al tries desperately to piece together the blurry scene. Despite being partially blind, she can still see Stefano's fuzzy moustache.

"Hang in there, Stefano." She smiles at him.

"You too, *bambina*," his hoarse voice replies.

They walk past a few more beds full of unidentifiable guards. Just before they exit the room, the faces on the beds turn to white cloth. *They must be the ones that died*, Al thinks to herself. They get outside into the damp, early morning air and Sonny takes in the horrible sight of smouldering buildings and people clearing through rubble to find more bodies.

"Sonny, watch out, there's a car!" Al warns her.

Despite being blind, the headlights burnt her eyeballs enough to notice it.

Sonny tugs her backwards out of the way of the car and laughs. "The blind leading the blind."

They rush into the car before any more accidents occur, and manoeuvre their way out of the bombsite that used to be the Fontana complex.

"Did people die?" Al asks, looking out the window at a blur of dark scenery.

"A few guards... and Calvino."

Al's mouth drops open and she turns to her sister. "Calvino's dead?"

"Yeah..."

Al shakes her head glumly. "RIP Calvino." She kisses her finger and points to the sky.

"We're lucky there aren't more," Sonny adds.

"Not that we know of. Everything will be clearer tomorrow."

"Including your vision, hopefully." Sonny tries to lighten the mood.

Al laughs weakly. "It couldn't get much worse."

They both manage to catch a few hours of sleep before the sun rises and the birds start to chirp. It was not the best night's sleep ever; Al had constant nightmares and Sonny couldn't switch off her brain, leaving them with only a couple of hours of rest before they felt obliged to go back to the complex and help out.

Their dad is already long gone to work and Karen is in the garden, pottering around and watering plants. Sonny goes into Al's room and wakes her up. Her eyes squint open and shut about a million times before she can finally unbolt them completely.

"Can you see me? How many fingers am I holding up?" Sonny asks, sticking her middle finger up at Al.

She looks on, unamused. "One."

"Aah, so you can see!"

"Yeah, your ugly mug," Al teases.

Sonny hits her on the arm playfully before getting down to business. "Shall we go to the complex then?"

Al nods solemnly.

"Get dressed then."

And that they do, climbing into the car fifteen minutes later. They get to the complex and the security on the front gate is ramped up. An armed guard approaches the driver side window.

"Name?" he barks.

"Al and Sonny Fontana."

He nods to another guard, who activates the gates to let them in. Sonny rolls the window up as they wait for a wide enough gap for the car to fit through.

"So, we're Fontanas now, are we?" Al smirks.

"Yeah, thought you knew that."

"It's cooler than Shelley, to be fair."

The entire clan is out in the complex, clearing up and rebuilding what they can, apart from The Don and his family. They pull up outside the mansion, where a new set of doors has been erected. Nobody comes to greet them, so they ring the bell and wait patiently. Mario answers, his face still full of sorrow.

"Sorry. Come in," he says quietly.

For some reason, the girls feel like they should make as little noise as possible, and so they tiptoe over the doorstep and gently take off their shoes.

"Are you okay, Mario?" Sonny asks him.

"I'm fine," he says, but his clenched jaw and quivering Adam's apple say differently.

The girls pull him into a group hug and they give him a comforting pat on the back. Al feels a tear drip onto the top of her head, which makes her hug him even tighter.

"Everyone's in the living room." He guides them there once they've untangled themselves from the embrace.

As they get closer, Alessa's wailing echoes dauntingly through the empty corridors. Suddenly, this mansion full of life and vibrancy is anything but, and all it took was a couple of fateful hours. Everybody is dressed in black, something the girls didn't anticipate. Luckily, they both dressed in dark clothes that morning; it's true that clothes reflect your emotions.

The Don leaves Alessa's side to greet the girls. "Thank you for coming," he says, holding out his arm for a handshake.

They ignore it and give him a hug instead. He hesitates at first, his hands hovering behind them, but he soon gives in; a hug can cure anything.

The girls can tell that the Fontanas are not a very physically embracing family; they are all sitting at a distance away from each other, only offering a hand on the shoulder as solace. The girls take it upon themselves to break these boundaries for them.

Sonny heads straight to Bella, who is sitting with her head in her hands, weeping. She sits down next to her and, with her arm around her shoulders, pulls her in towards her. Bella relaxes her head on her shoulder and cries into a tissue.

Al decides Alessa needs comfort the most and so bypasses everyone else to sit with her. "I'm so sorry, Alessa. I wish there was something we could do," she says, rubbing Alessa's back gently.

"Me too. He didn't deserve this; he was a good boy," she weeps, her words barely understandable.

The Don comes to join them again, perching on the other side of his wife.

"*Vi porgo le mie più sentite condoglianze.*" (I offer you my most heartfelt condolences.)

Alessa sniffs and wipes her teary eyes with a tissue, appreciating the use of her mother tongue. "*Grazie, amore mio,*" she says, and takes hold of Al's

146

hand. They smile solemnly at each other until Alessa can't hold her tears back any longer and crumples back into herself, bringing the tissue up to her face again.

The Don looks around the room at his crying family, and although he feels the same terrible sadness as everybody else, he only sees this as a distraction from the bigger picture: They were raided by a SWAT team! He stands to address the room.

"Everybody, *mia famiglia*. We cannot let this loss affect us. We are under attack, and we must fight back! We are stronger than this. We will not show them weakness," he begins and everybody listens quietly. "Yes, we have lost a son, a brother... But we have gained two daughters." He motions to Al and Sonny. "Calvino did not die for nothing, he died for *us*, his family, our cause. Let us not let him down. We will avenge him."

As the realisation sinks in and the tears dry up, a fiery determination ignites inside everybody in the room. They will continue on, in Calvino's honour. Now, every mission and every killing will have a much deeper meaning. This is for family.

"We will hold his funeral this week. After that... I will hear no more about it. *Capisci?*" The Don demands.

The room is silent. This seems like a big ask from Don Fontana and nobody wants to reply on behalf of everybody.

"*Sì*," Alessa whimpers.

He nods. "*Buono.*"

The Don takes a deep breath and exits the room. The tears have stopped now, and everybody looks at each other in bemusement.

"I'll go and make some food. You all must be hungry," Alessa says, hurrying to the kitchen before anyone can protest.

Al looks over at Luca, who she hasn't seen crying yet. "You okay, Luca?" she asks him.

He nods quickly and offers a weak smile.

She bites her lip. "I'll be back in a second." She gets up from the sofa and exits the room.

As Al wanders through the corridors, she can hear Alessa crying again, but she decides to leave her on her own for now; she has another destination in mind. She gives two gentle knocks on the door.

"Yes?"

"It's Al, can I come in?"

"*Sì.*"

She pries open one of the doors and slowly steps into the office. The Don is sitting behind his desk with a tumbler of whisky in his hand. Even from the doorway, she can see he has been crying.

"Can I sit?"

"Of course." He waves her to the seat in front of the desk.

"How are you doing?"

He nods. "I am fine. It is my wife I worry about."

"I'm sure she worries about you, too."

"There is no need. I am ready to continue business."

She pulls out a pack of cigarettes. "Smoke?"

He accepts and they sit together silently for a moment as they breathe in the first lungful of smoke, uninterrupted.

"I have something to propose to you. You may not like it, though," Al explains.

His interest is piqued. "What is it?"

"I think we should talk with the Baulsacks."

His face hardens. "The Germans? Why?"

"Well, we could work together. They need Holdis back, we need the police gone. And we both know they would turn their back on the force."

"I don't know, Al. They are a very dangerous bunch."

"That's why we'd do it on our turf."

He shakes his head. "I'm not sure. I'll think about it."

"Extreme times cause for extreme measures." She shrugs.

"I understand what you're saying. But doesn't your father work for the police?"

"I don't think you are understanding." She stares at him, trying to get the message across.

The Don nods slowly. "I will have a plan ready for two days' time, I will brief everybody together, we don't need help from any *tudro*."

"Alright."

The Don looks off blankly in the distance. It takes a while for him to speak, but Al waits patiently. "He was the best kid anyone could ask for. It is my fault he's dead."

"Don't say that..."

"But it is. He didn't want anything to do with this side of the business. I started this to give my children a better life than I had, and now he has no life at all."

Al sighs. "He was protecting your business, he knew what he was doing."

The Don stubs out his cigarette aggressively.

"Tell me some stories about him."

He grumbles and clears his throat. "He was our second born. He and Mario were like polar opposites, one had pitch-black hair, the other was bald." He laughs. "He got bullied terribly at school for it, until Mario caught wind. He went into class and beat up every kid that ever said anything bad about Vino. He was never bullied after that."

Al chuckles along with the story.

"He was a great older brother to the other three. Mario not so much, he should have beaten himself up with how much he bullied his poor siblings. But Calvino, he was caring and considerate. His sisters used to love dressing him up in crazy costumes, and he didn't mind because it meant he got to wear a wig."

Al and The Don both burst out laughing just

thinking about it. He wipes a tear from his eye as he chuckles.

"He was very interested in cooking, always helping out his mother in the kitchen. That's why I gave him control over Fonty's, it was his passion. He was perhaps the friendliest member of the family; he did anything for anyone."

"I know I didn't know him that well, but I can believe everything you're telling me. He did seem like a great guy."

"I wish you'd had more time to get to know him." The Don nods sadly.

"I'll make up for it with the other four. It's about time we all started bonding."

"I believe you've already begun with Zeta," he says, looking up suspiciously.

Al shifts in her seat. "You've heard?"

"I have."

"We meant no harm. She swung for Sonny first, we were just protecting ourselves."

He chuckles gruffly. "Don't worry, she needs putting in her place sometimes. I wish I could hit her myself from time to time."

Al smiles now. "We'll be on standby, then."

He laughs and walks around the desk. Al rises to meet him. He puts his hand on her shoulder. "*Grazie di tutto, amore mio.* Let's go back and join everybody, this is a time to be together, no?"

The entire family swarms to Manchester to say their farewells to Calvino. Because it was such short notice, The Don paid for flights for everyone from all around the world so that they could attend. The Van De Jaagers have also turned up to pay their respects to Don Fontana; even the Italian Mafia family in London have travelled up.

Al and Sonny have never seen a funeral with so many people before, and it isn't all doom and gloom, they can hear laughing and friendly chatter between the guests. The funeral is being held in the complex. A giant marquee has been set up and a Catholic priest is present to undertake the ceremony. There are graves already in a remote corner of the complex, Alessa's mother's being one of them.

Everyone in the immediate family is wearing a tailored black suit made by Alessa, who stayed up all night to finish them, but she mostly just wanted to distract herself from what is to come. The girls stand with the Fontanas and greet anyone who approaches. Nonna is pushed over to them in a wheelchair. The skin on her hands is a dark purple, and if it weren't for the black tights, her legs would look the same. One by one, the family bends down to kiss her cheeks and wish her well.

"Is she okay?" Al whispers to Mario.

He leans closer. "She injured herself when she was rushing to get out of the complex."

Al puts her hand on her heart. "Poor Nonna," she says with pure sadness.

"She'll be okay." Mario smiles.

Suddenly, Mario nudges her on the arm. He tilts across Al to address Sonny as well. "This is Calvino's wife. She has no idea about the business so don't say anything," he whispers.

"Wife? I didn't know he was married!" Sonny says in surprise.

Mario shrugs. "She lives in Italy, they hardly knew they were married themselves."

A young woman, wearing a black veil and long, silk gloves, strides towards the family. She is clutching a handkerchief and a small black handbag covered in diamonds.

"*Buona sera, famiglia. Suocero,*" she greets them, and bows her head to her father-in-law. (Good evening, family. Father-in-law.)

"*Ciao, Sofia. Come sta la tua famiglia in Italia?*" The Don enquires about her family back home as the rest of the Fontanas listen patiently.

"*Benissimo, grazie,*" she says, holding the handkerchief up to her sodden cheek.

She spots the two unusual-looking girls at the end of the line of family members. She frowns at them in confusion.

"Al and Sonny," Al shouts over, with a smile and a nod.

"*Inglese?*" she asks The Don, even more confused now.

He shrugs, with a smirk; they may be English, but they probably know Italian better than he does. The Don guides her into the marquee, and tells her they'll be in soon. She leaves reluctantly, glancing back at the girls a few times before she disappears into the tent.

"What's up with her?" Al asks.

"I doubt she's ever met an English person, her family live way out in the countryside. I wouldn't worry about it." Mario shrugs it off.

"*Daar zijn ze!*" (There they are!) a booming voice shouts from across the patch of grass. Everybody turns to see who the foreigner is. It's Casper. His dad slaps him on the arm and tells him to be respectful

As they get closer, Don Van De Jaager rolls his eyes and apologises to Don Fontana as they shake hands. Jelle makes his way over to the girls, who are happy to see him.

"Hey, guys. I wish we were meeting under happier circumstances," he says, as he shakes their hands, as well as Mario and Luca's. "Vino was a great guy."

"He really was," Mario replies.

Casper walks over and joins them. "Luca.

Klootzaks," he insults Mario and the girls. (Motherfuckers.)

Mario looks to the girls for what that means. Al looks up at him. "You don't wanna know."

"What're you even doing 'ere?" Sonny asks him, her northern accent getting stronger with contempt.

"I've come to pay my respects." He shrugs obnoxiously.

"Your respect means nothing," Mario tells him.

Casper dramatically clutches at his chest. "Ouch."

"Just go away, Casper, you're not helping anyone. Especially not yourself," Jelle snaps.

Al raises her eyebrows in surprised pride at Jelle speaking up to his brother. "You 'eard the man, get lost."

Casper looks around at everyone. They all look back at him, amused. He deserved that, and much more. He says nothing and returns to his dad's side, scowling at them all.

"Sorry about him. I don't know why he bothered coming." Jelle shakes his head in disappointment.

"Don't worry. At least we can kick him out if he carries on."

"Jelle! We're going in," Aart shouts over to his son.

He nods to his friends. "See you in there."

The Van De Jaagers join the other mourners in the marquee. Last to arrive are the Southern Italians.

They pull up in a black Rolls Royce. Once the car comes to a stop, the driver gets out and opens the door for whoever is sitting in the back. A stylish young Italian woman is helped out of the limo and two young men let themselves out of the other doors. The tallest man approaches the family with arms outstretched.

"Fontanas. I'm so sorry about your loss, no one deserves to lose a son so young," he says, embracing Alessa and kissing her cheeks before moving on to The Don.

The man is Matteo Russo. He is the leader of the family since his father was shot by the Baulsack Mafia last year. He is tall, not particularly well-built, but he is a very clever man and makes sure he has other people who can do the dirty work for him. One of those is his brother, Salvadore, the other young man accompanying them. He is of average height and walks with swagger and arrogance, your typical Italian gangster.

The young woman is Matteo's wife, Valentina. She is blissfully unaware of what her husband gets up to, but still, she loves spending his dirty money on clothes and jewellery. She stands close to her husband and doesn't greet anybody; she merely looks them all up and down in disdain, as if she is better than everyone here.

Salvadore nods at Mario from a distance and he reciprocates the acknowledgment. He checks Al and

Sonny out, chewing on his toothpick. He isn't unattractive, but he emits the feeling of being a sleazeball, which makes the girls' skin crawl. Al grimaces towards Sonny, out of Salvadore's sight; Sonny laughs and nods slyly in agreement.

Once everyone has been greeted, the family file into the front of the marquee and the ceremony begins. The Don presents his eulogy and there isn't a dry eye among the family members; everyone sits in silent, mournful reflection. One by one, people step up to the open casket to kiss Calvino's cheeks for the last time.

His wife, Sofia, is there for the longest time, hugging his cold body and kissing every inch of his face. Afterwards, the crowd gathers around the grave site and they watch the long casket being lowered into the ground. People throw flowers on top of the coffin before it gets covered in handfuls of fresh soil.

After the funeral, a lavish party of sorts is thrown. Guests have brought over food, as is the tradition in Italy, and the guests come together to feast on the offerings. Tables are set up around the grounds and people mingle and eat wherever they please. The girls are at a table with Mario, Luca, Bella and Jelle.

"Where's Bente?" Bella asks him.

"She stayed home with our mother," Jelle explains.

"Aw, that's a shame. I would have loved to have seen her again."

"I can imagine you two getting on," Sonny says, with a smile.

Bella turns to her. "Why do you say that?"

"You both seem very similar people," she explains, and sees Jelle smirk out of the corner of her eye.

"We get on." Bella shrugs.

Al looks around at the others guests and she spots The Don sitting with Matteo and Salvadore Russo, talking quickly and fervently. Matteo looks at his wife and then back to The Don, then they stand up abruptly, followed by Salvadore and they start towards the house. As they pass the table, The Don orders Al, Sonny, Mario and Luca to join them in the office, as well as ordering Jelle to retrieve his father.

"Why do those two get to go and I don't?" Bella scowls at her dad, referring to Al and Sonny.

"Because, my beautiful Bella, you've got your own mission."

She perks up now. "What is it?"

"Keep Mrs Russo company," he says, pointing towards the woman on her own.

Bella's face drops to an agitated frown again. She pushes her chair back forcefully without breaking eye contact with her dad, and wanders over to Valentina, plastering a fake smile across her face.

The three families all crowd into the office, grabbing a drink and a cigarette before they get down to business.

"I said I wouldn't do business today. However, this has been brought to me twice now and we must address it as a family," The Don explains, pouring himself a whisky.

"What is it?" Luca asks worriedly.

"Al came to me yesterday and suggested a meeting with the Baulsacks." Everyone turns to look at her with confused expressions.

"Keep listening," Al urges them.

"Our friend Matteo also suggested this, however, with a difference."

Salvadore interrupts with a smirk to finish the story. "Kill 'em all."

The Don stares silently for a moment. "Yes."

"They're all over the place, how would we do that?"

"Get them all in one place, like a meeting." Al nods at The Don, who nods back.

Mario sits forward to see everyone. "Under what premise? They'd never agree to meet us."

"We'll tell them we want to abolish the police force, and we need their help to do it."

Mario grimaces at the thought of even asking the Baulsacks for help.

"I know, son. But they're slowly raking in more

and more enemies, so it's us against them. We'll have every Mafia family in the world behind us."

Mario looks at Luca, who just shrugs. He sees no problem with it so far. Don Van de Jaager nods in agreement with Don Fontana's utterance. Mario takes a big drag of his cigarette whilst he thinks about it.

"Come on, Mario. *Non fare il pappamolla, amico,*" Salvadore mocks him, with a smug look on his face. (Don't be a wuss, man.)

"I haven't said I won't do it." He scowls at having been called a wimp.

"Calm down. We can work on it more another time. All we need to know for now is that everybody is in favour of doing this."

They all nod, some reluctantly.

"Great, then we'll be in touch," The Don says, holding his hand out for Matteo to shake.

"*Grazie,* Don," Matteo says, gripping his hand tightly.

Salvadore and Aart shake his hand, too, and everyone exits the study together.

Mario hangs back to talk to his old friend.

"Salva, you're looking as sly as usual," Mario says, patting him on the back.

"You know me, Mario." He smirks and lets out a dirty laugh. "So, them girls, who are they?"

Mario clears his throat, knowing what's coming.

"Al and Sonny. They're part of the family now, so no, you can't have your way with either of them."

"It's too late for Bella." Salva sniggers.

Mario's face hardens to a bone-chilling glare.

Salva shrugs nonchalantly. "What? It's true."

Mario pushes him into the hard corner of the doorframe and Salva moans in pain but doesn't put up a fight.

"Don't disrespect my family." Mario spits in his face.

Salva holds his hands up in surrender, his face still covered in a mocking smile.

"Everything alright?" Al pops her head around the corner.

Mario quickly lets go of Salva and neatens up his suit.

"Yes, we're fine. We're just play-fighting like old times, eh, Salva?"

"Oh, yes." He nods. "*Non mi dispiacerebbe giocare con lei,*" Salva says to Al, so to annoy Mario even more. (I wouldn't mind playing with her.)

Al grimaces. "Ew. *Nei tuoi sogni.*" (In your dreams.)

Mario laughs. "Did I mention they speak Italian?"

Salva gathers up his ego. "No, you didn't tell me that." He glares.

Al shoots him a sarcastic smile and waves goodbye before slipping back behind the wall.

"So, what's the deal with you two?"

Mario looks at him in surprise. "What? Nothing," he says quickly.

Salva raises his eyebrow. "If you don't, I will." He winks and pushes past him.

Outside, Valentina is rejoined by her husband and brother-in-law. Mario searches for any familiar face to talk to. He spots Al and Jelle disappearing inside the house via a side door and strides towards them to find out where they're going, but he is halted in his tracks when he nearly falls over a weeping Sofia, so small she wasn't even in his line of vision.

"Sofia, I'm so sorry, I didn't see you there," he apologises in Italian, the only language she understands.

"It's okay, Mario." She sniffs. "I miss him so much."

Mario sighs. It's time to slow down. He puts his arms around her. "Don't worry, you'll still be taken care of," he tells her, his eyes on the side door still.

"It's not that. He used to write me letters, you know? He had a beautiful heart."

"He did," he agrees, becoming more impatient by the minute.

He manages to make eye contact with Sonny, who is sitting flirting with Bella. He pushes his eyes wide open to say 'save me!' and Sonny thankfully cottons on.

She wanders over. "Hey, Mario, can I talk to you for a minute?"

"Oh, of course, Sonny. Excuse me, Sofia," he says, kissing her on the cheek.

Mario and Sonny walk a few steps away from her before speaking.

"What's up?" Sonny asks.

"Where's Al? I need to apologise to her about what happened before," he explains.

Sonny frowns. "What happened before?"

"Nothing. Just Salva being an idiot as usual," he says, still looking around to see if Al has emerged yet.

"She went inside with Jelle."

"What are they doing?" he asks quickly.

Sonny smirks. "Don't get jealous, Mario," she says, hitting him lightly on the arm.

Bella joins the conversation. "Who's he jealous of now?"

"Shut up, Bella." He rolls his eyes.

"What's your problem?"

"Did you sleep with Salva?" he questions his sister.

She looks astonished. "What?"

"Did you?" He raises his voice a bit now.

"No!" she lies.

Mario shakes his head. "Don't lie to me, I know you did. He told me."

Bella pulls a disgusted face. "You're not jealous of Salva, are you?" She looks her brother up and down.

It's Mario's turn to shake his head in disgust. "*Che cazzo.*" He spits, and storms off towards the house. (What the fuck.)

Bella and Sonny grin at each other mischievously. "I love winding him up."

Mario starts by checking all the downstairs rooms but there is no sight of the pair. He rushes down corridors, bumping into guests on his way, including one of his uncles,

"Mario, what is wrong?" he asks in his thick Italian accent.

"Why are there so many fucking rooms in this house?" he shouts, not looking back to address his uncle properly.

He gets to the top of the stairs and spots two figures seated on the lounge chairs on the main balcony. He quickly pushes the door open to surprise them. He expects them to jump and look back guiltily, but they don't. Instead, Al slowly turns to look at him.

"Alright, Mario?" She smiles, her eyes looking droopy.

"What are you doing up here?" he asks sternly.

Jelle turns around now and holds the spliff up to show him. "Want some?"

He quickly calms down and silently takes the spliff from him, taking a long drag.

"I was looking everywhere for you," he says to Al.

"Oh, is something wrong?"

He takes a moment to answer. "No." He shakes his head, looking from Al to Jelle quickly.

"I better go and make sure my brother isn't causing havoc. I'll see you later," Jelle announces, standing up from the chair.

"Thanks for the weed." Al smiles and the two fist-bump each other before he closes the balcony door behind him.

Mario leans against the hefty stone balcony in front of Al as he finishes the spliff off.

"Everything okay?" she asks cautiously.

"Yeah," he quips, but his gaze says otherwise.

Al sighs. "Go on, tell me."

He shrugs. "I just didn't like the way Salva spoke to you before."

"I've had worse, don't worry."

He throws the end of the spliff off the balcony and sits down next to Al.

He explains hurriedly, without thinking about what he's saying, "I know, but he's been doing this to me for years. As soon as he knows I like someone, he tries to get in between."

They both look at each other and slowly, a smirk cuts across Al's face. Soon enough, they're both laughing, partly out of embarrassment, partly because they're stoned. After the chuckles have stopped, Mario rubs his face with his hands and turns to her again, more relaxed this time.

"Sorry, that just came out."

"Don't worry about it." She pats him on the leg. "And F-Y-I, I'd pick you over that minger any day."

He looks at the ground. "Good to know."

"Shall we go back outside?"

"Yeah." He stands and holds out his hand for Al, and they rejoin the party.

———

"Did you really shag Salva?" Sonny asks Bella, with a disgusted look on her face.

She shrugs. "Maybe."

"But he's so gross."

"No, he isn't! Have you seen him?" She lovingly glances over to the table he's sitting at.

"Unfortunately, yeah. You could do so much better than that."

Bella quickly turns to look at her. "Like who?"

They study each other's faces intently.

Sonny shrugs. "Dunno."

"Like you?" Bella raises her eyebrows.

"If that's what you're into, I don't see why not." She laughs.

Out of nowhere, Casper pokes his head in between their faces.

"Hello, beautiful." He smiles, right in Bella's face. He then turns to Sonny. "Hello, Sonny."

"What do you want?" Bella asks sternly.

He straightens up and stands next to Bella. "I

came over to see if you'd like to go on a stroll with me." He holds out his hand for her to take.

She looks at it mockingly. "No thanks. I'm gonna stay here with my girlfriend." She smiles and takes hold of Sonny's hand instead.

Casper frowns. "Girlfriend?"

"You heard it here first." Sonny smiles at Bella.

"Whatever." He shakes his head and walks off in a paddy.

After they've watched him stomp around for a bit, Sonny turns back to Bella. "So, I'm your girlfriend now?"

She laughs. "Just while Casper's here."

"CASPER, COME BACK!" she shouts, but not loud enough for him to hear.

Bella cracks up into laughter. "You're so funny," she tells Sonny. They both stare at each other with a wanting look in their eyes.

The rest of the night is a bit of a blur for the girls as the more guests that leave, the more booze they consume. As soon as the sun beams through the thin white curtains in the Fontana mansion, Al gathers her belongings and sneaks out of the room, leaving Mario fast asleep in bed. She slowly and quietly closes the door behind her. As she turns, she spots

Sonny doing exactly the same thing further down the corridor.

They look at each other and wave, with big smiles. They both wander out of the front door and get into the car.

"Whose room were you in? Not Luca's!" Al laughs.

Sonny laughs, too. "Nah."

"Who then?"

"I don't kiss and tell, mate."

"It was Bella, wasn't it?" Al smirks.

Sonny doesn't reply but the guilty look on her face says it all.

"Ahh, it was! *NOICE!*" Al teases her.

Sonny tries not to laugh. "You're such an idiot."

They get home and they're greeted in the front room by their dad. It's the first time they've seen him in days.

"Where've you two been? You look like you've been to a funeral." He frowns at their fancy but macabre outfits.

"Don't I always?" Sonny says, to get out of it; it's very seldom that she isn't wearing black.

"True." Shelley laughs weakly.

"How's work been, Dad?" Al asks.

He shakes his head and sighs. "Horrible. There's

a huge conflict of interest at the minute."

"With what?"

"I can't talk about it too much, but they planned an attack on one of the Mafia families. Every single one of the SWAT team died, and a few Mafia members. There's going to be a shit storm," he explains, starting to bite his nails now.

The girls sit either side of their dad,

"What about the detective that died in Wales?" Sonny asks cautiously.

"No evidence. They reckoned it was the work of the family they ambushed. Which, even if it was, doing that would just make the situation one hundred times worse, which they have!"

Al rubs his back gently. "What happens now then?"

"I'm not sure, they're keeping me out of it. I'm too strait-laced."

Sonny shrugs. "Maybe you should just quit."

He sits up to look at her. "And do what? I'm the only one making money."

"We can get a job," Sonny suggests.

"No." Shelley stands up. "I can't have that. I'm just going to do what I can and bite my lip when needed."

He turns to the front door. "I need to go to work."

"But it's a Saturday."

"They need all the help they can get at the moment."

CHAPTER TWELVE

T he following Monday, Al and Sonny return to Fonty's for the first time since being held hostage in there. A big black and white picture of Calvino has been framed in front of the entrance for everyone to see. Al kisses her fingers and presses them against the frame. Sonny follows suit. They wander further into the establishment and see some members of the Fontanas sitting in a booth with the Russo clan.

"Alright?" Al greets them, before swiftly sitting down.

"Hey, guys. Come, we've only just started," Don Fontana urges.

Sonny sits down next to Al and waits patiently for them to begin.

"So far, we have decided the meeting will take place here. Everyone here will be present."

That means that Al, Sonny, Mario, Luca, Bella, Salva, Matteo and The Don will all have a part to play in this mission.

"What about the Van De Jaagers?" Sonny asks.

The Don shakes his head. "They're too well-known to the Germans; they'll realise something is going on."

"Are they going to help?"

"Of course. They'll be holding their own meeting in Amsterdam, so half of the Baulsacks will be there and the rest will be here. We're taking care of things separately, as Aart and I agreed."

"So, what's the plan?" Salva probes impatiently.

The Don nods towards Al and Luca. "That's for these two to decide."

Al and Luca both raise their eyebrows at each other. "The dream team." Al winks.

"She's the brains?" Matteo asks The Don in Italian.

"*Lei parla Italiano,*" Salva tells his brother uninterestedly as he fiddles with his watch. (She speaks Italian.)

Matteo quickly turns to Al, who smiles awkwardly at him.

"Don't make the same mistake so many of us have by underestimating these two girls." The Don points to Al and Sonny. "They're much more intelligent than we are," he tells him sternly.

"I apologise." Matteo bows his head out of respect, "But I assure you, I never make the same mistake twice."

"Great. Then we'll get on with the planning."

Al and Luca leave the table and head into the staffroom at the back of the building.

They go back and forth for hours, trying to think of a non-intimidating scenario to lure the Baulsacks into the restaurant and kill them before they even realise what's going on. Eventually, they manage to agree on a plan.

As they come back into the main area of the restaurant, they find that the sky is now dull and everyone is either playing games on their phone or asleep across the booths. Salva's head is dangling out of the closest booth.

Al decides to announce the plan's completion in the best way she knows how; she sneaks up beside Salva and shouts, "DONE!" right next to his ear. He lets out a very feminine scream and jumps out of the booth. Everyone bursts out laughing, even The Don, who Al thought would be her toughest critic.

"What the hell was that for?" Salva shouts angrily.

"Just checking you're still alive."

He nods, wide-eyed. "I was until you nearly killed me."

"Alright, enough." The Don sniggers. "Let's hear what you've got."

Salva swiftly pulls the two sides of his blazer back together before sitting down in the booth, where everyone re-joins him.

Luca begins to explain.

"So, we invite them here to talk about eradicating the police. We go along with it, offer them anything they want, give them a really good deal. Then, at the very end, we poison them with food made here."

"And how are we gonna do that without them knowing?" Matteo asks, not having much faith in this plan.

"We'll all have the same meal, but we'll use different plates for the Baulsacks. A slight enough difference for us to notice, but not them," Al explains.

Everyone looks at The Don. He nods. "It can work. Well done, you two."

Matteo and Salva look at each other cautiously.

"It took you that long to come up with that?" Salva asks condescendingly.

"What's *your* plan?" Al frowns at him.

He becomes twitchy and his eyes search everybody's face. "Plans aren't my forte." He shrugs.

"Shut up then."

Salva looks at The Don, expecting him to stand up for him, but he merely smirks and shrugs at him in reply. Salva shakes his head angrily and Matteo taps him on the arm to get back into the car. They all shake hands and The Don assures them he'll make the call tomorrow and will let them know the verdict as soon as he finds out.

As The Don sees the Russos out, Mario sneaks over to Al.

"Hey." He grins.

She looks up at him. "Alright?"

"We haven't had a chance to talk all night," he points out.

"Is there something you need to say?"

He shrugs one of his shoulders. "Not particularly, I just thought, after the other night..."

She stares back at him.

He frowns and lowers his voice. "Have I done something to upset you?"

"Just keeping things professional," she states.

"Come on, Al. We're going home," Sonny shouts to her from the entrance.

Al holds out a hand for Mario to shake, which he does, reluctantly.

"Be seeing you," she tells him, before exiting the building.

Once The Don is back in the comfort of his own home, with a belly full of homemade food and warming alcohol, he slinks off to his office to talk to Don Baulsack. He lowers himself into his soft leather office chair, lights a cigar with a match and puffs on it a few times, before pouring himself another whisky. He gathers his thoughts first, sipping and smoking as he looks around the room, at the ornate ceiling, the cabinet-covered walls, but not seeing anything in particular. He blows out a final gust of smoke before taking the phone off the receiver.

He flicks through his address book, his finger searching the page full of surnames beginning with 'B', finally landing on *Baulsack, H.* He dials in the numbers and sits in silence, listening to the ominous ringing propelling out of the earpiece. It seems to go on forever, until suddenly, the ringing stops.

"Mr Holdis Baulsack's office, who is calling, please?" a young-sounding German woman answers.

"Hello, my darling. I am Don Fontana, I have some urgent business to discuss with your employer," he tells her, in his clearest voice.

"One moment." The phone clicks silent.

The Don takes this opportunity to have some more drink. He notices the ice in his tumbler is rattling against the glass. He doesn't feel nervous, but he is shaking.

"Don Fontana, to what do I owe the pleasure?" The hard, German voice booms with resentment and sarcasm.

"Don Baulsack. I know it has been a long time since we have spoken."

"Not long enough," he grumbles.

"I disagree. Now is a better time than any," The Don starts.

"And why is that, *Don Fontana*?" He draws out the name.

The Don lets out a smoke-filled sigh before explaining, "I have heard about your brother... "

Don Baulsack interrupts curtly. "What about my brother?"

"That he was taken in by those bastards."

The line goes quiet as Don Baulsack re-evaluates the meaning of this call.

"Go on," he prompts curiously.

"Recently, they raided our complex and... killed my son." He clears his throat. "We are finally ready to fight back."

"But you need our help," Don Baulsack figures.

The Don nods to himself. "Exactly."

"Hmm..." He ponders the thought. "Let me think about it."

"What could persuade you to arrive this week?" Don Fontana pushes.

"What are you offering?"

The Don sighs quietly at the thought of having to say what he is about to. "Whatever you want. We are at your mercy, Don Baulsack. We cannot defeat them without you and your men."

"What is your territory?" the voice on the other end asks, becoming softer and more in control.

"The whole of the north of England... Some in the Midlands."

"I'll take whatever you have in the Midlands, plus a share in all your drug operations."

The Don lets out a more audible sigh now, performing for Baulsack. "I wouldn't agree if I weren't so desperate... We have a deal, Don Baulsack."

A raspy chuckle rattles into The Don's ears, so much so that he pulls the phone away from his head.

"I'll talk to my men and inform you of our arrival. Pleasure doing business with you, *Don*." The German hangs up the phone.

"Smug bastard," The Don mutters under his breath.

He returns to the living room where Mario and Luca are waiting eagerly to hear from their father.

"Well?" Luca asks.

"He agreed." The Don nods.

"You don't look happy about it." Mario points out.

The Don shakes his head. "He is taking us for fools."

Luca stands up and puts his hand on his father's broad shoulder. "In the end, they'll be the fools."

CHAPTER THIRTEEN

The next day, Don Van de Jaager picks up his phone and dials the number quickly, and without having to look in his address book.

"Mr Holdis Baulsack's office, how may I help you?" the same sweet voice asks.

"Don Van de Jaager."

"One moment." The line goes silent.

"Aart, my friend! How have you been?"

The voice takes him by surprise. "Ah, Holdis. I've been well, friend, and yourself?"

"*Wunderbar!*"

"If you don't mind me asking... is it to do with the Fontanas?"

Don Baulsack's voice becomes sterner now. "What do you know?"

"He called me last night. About eradicating the police there."

"What did he offer you?" Baulsack presses aggressively.

"I didn't accept."

"Why not?"

"I saw opportunity."

"For what?" Baulsack probes.

"For us two."

"... What do you have in mind?"

Tonight, the Fontanas invite Al and Sonny over for dinner. It's been a while since they've been round. The repairs on the complex were finally completed this week, bringing the bustling village back to its former Roman glory. The security is higher than ever, but thankfully the girls are known well enough now to enter unchallenged.

Their first stop is in the kitchen, with Alessa, sampling the tapas plates she's put together.

"You're the real Don, Alessa, you've been cheated out of that one," Al jokes, once she's had her fill of exotically named food.

Alessa smiles. "Speaking of The Don, I think he wanted to speak to you both before dinner. He should be in his office with the boys."

"Sure you don't need any help?" Sonny asks, already halfway out the door.

Alessa laughs, knowing she doesn't mean it. "Oh, actually, you could peel some potatoes for me..."

Sonny sighs, wishing she hadn't asked, but she begins walking over to the island again.

Alessa stops her. "I'm joking, darling." She waves her back out the door. "Attend to your own business."

"Thank God!" Sonny laughs, hand on heart.

The girls knock on the office door and let themselves in. Only Zeta and Alessa aren't present.

"Hey, guys." They smile to everyone as they take a seat.

"Good evening, ladies," The Don greets them. "Now we're all here, let us discuss the plan for this week."

"Have you managed to speak to Helmut, then?" Al asks.

The Don nods. "Yes. He agreed to meet under the pretence of acquiring our territory in the Midlands."

"The Russos own the majority, so they won't be happy when they find out," Luca adds.

"It's not like we're actually going to hand it over, though," Mario scoffs.

Bella rolls her eyes. "Who cares about the Russos, anyway?"

"You, apparently." Mario grimaces.

"Enough." The Don calmly nips the argument in

the bud. "They will be informed and they will be okay with it," he says, with an air of dominance and power that gives the girls goosebumps.

"Have you spoken to Don Van de Jaager?" Al asks The Don.

He shakes his head. "Not since our initial call, but I'm sure he's busy preparing for his own meeting."

They all nod silently.

"I have something to show you!" Luca says, jumping up from his seat.

He leaves the room momentarily and returns with a large cardboard box that rattles with every step he takes. He places it on the big glass coffee table in the middle of the office and uses one of his father's letter openers to slice the Sellotape enclosing the contents of the box.

"*Voilà!*" He sings, taking a plate, that says 'Fonty's' around the edges, out of the box and showing it to everyone.

"Wow, a plate," Bella says unamused.

"Not just any plate," Luca starts, "this is a poisonous plate." He smiles menacingly.

Mario takes the plate from Luca. "It's got poison on it?"

"No... See if you can tell the difference," he says, passing him another one from out of the box.

Mario studies them both for a while. "There is no difference..."

He passes the plates to Al and Sonny, who both scrutinise them intensely.

"One is missing an apostrophe," Al points out.

"*Corrrrrrrect!*" Luca shouts, like a gameshow host.

Mario frowns. "What's an apostrophe?"

It is a dark, foggy night in Manchester when the Baulsacks arrive via their private jet. The plane awaits their return, as they expect the meeting to be over swiftly. Fonty's is all set up; Al and Sonny are sitting in the back office, observing the restaurant through the CCTV cameras inside and listening in via the microphone attached to Luca.

The Fontana family are waiting nervously for their guests in a velvet booth, while the Russos are patiently hiding in a building in front of the restaurant, ready to snipe anyone who manages to get away.

Zeta has been roped into cooking and serving the meals tonight, she's doing it for Vino, just this once. She knows the plan; three plates for the Baulsacks, which are missing apostrophes in 'Fonty's', and the rest for everybody else.

A car pulls up outside the dimly-lit restaurant,

"Is everybody ready?" The Don asks.

"Ready," everyone able to reply confirms.

A group of bodyguards surround the car door, but nothing can help to conceal the beast of a German who's just risen from the back seat. The bodyguards enter first; they look around the building, checking for anything suspicious before allowing Helmut to enter.

The Don walks over to greet him, an arm outstretched for a handshake. One of the guards halts him abruptly before frisking his body for weapons, and perhaps with too much force, as he stumbles backwards a little bit.

"Sorry, Marco. It's protocol." Baulsack shrugs.

The Don tries to suppress his annoyance. "Not to worry. I can assure you nobody is armed."

"Your assurance is nothing," Helmut says gently, pushing past The Don. "Search everybody else!" he orders the guards.

The rest of the Fontanas stand to meet him and allow the guards to search them as they do so,

"You must be Mario," Baulsack says as he sizes him up.

He nods. "That's me."

"Last time I saw you, you were this high." He holds his hand low to the floor. "Are you still pissing and shitting yourself?" He laughs.

Mario grits his teeth. "Not for a couple of years now." He tries to join in with the joke.

Helmut throws his head back and lets out a roar of laughter, his belly jumping up and down with each splutter. "Comedian!" he says to his guards and points to Mario.

"Which one are you, Calvino? Is that a wig?" he asks Luca, and moves to touch his hair.

Luca pulls away. "Calvino is dead. I'm Luca."

"Ah... yes, I heard about that." He seems to be genuine for a moment, until he spies Bella.

"RRRR," he rolls his tongue. "I know exactly who you are, my Bella."

"*Lo ammazzo cazzo!*" (I'll fucking kill him!) Mario spits, his hands so tightly clenched in a fist, they've turned white.

"Mario!" The Don shouts to him as he walks over to join them. "*Pazienza.*" The Don puts a hand on his shoulder.

Mario relaxes under his touch and slumps back down into the booth.

"Let's get down to business, shall we?" The Don suggests, motioning for everybody to sit down.

"Actually," Helmut protests, "I have a special guest who is yet to arrive."

The Fontanas look at each other nervously.

"He's here," one of the guards tells Helmut in a low voice.

The front door opens, letting in a gust of freezing cold air that gives everybody shivers. None other than Aart Van de Jaager strolls through the restaurant. The Fontanas are really panicking now; this was not part of the plan.

"Aart," The Don tries not to sound too surprised, "what are you doing here?"

"I decided to go into business with Helmut at last," he explains.

The Don nods, disappointment on his face. "Is that so."

"It is so!" Helmut bellows, "Now, we are ready for business." He smiles annoyingly.

———

"Is that Aart?" Al asks, astonished.

Sonny leans closer to the screen. "It looks like it."

"What the fuck is going on?" Al says, as she flips out her phone to call Matteo.

He answers on the first ring. "What's up?"

"I wish I knew. It looks like Aart has teamed up with Helmut."

"That wasn't part of the plan, was it?"

"Nope."

"Well, keep me updated, we're on standby," Matteo says, before hanging up the call.

Al turns her attention back to the screen,

"God, you can tell he's lovin' it." She grimaces at Helmut's smug face.

"How has he managed to sway Aart?" Sonny ponders aloud.

———

"So, it's settled." Helmut begins to conclude the meeting. "Aart and I will take over your territory in the Midlands, as well as the opportunity to traffic drugs and women across the country. We will also be taking a fifty percent cut of any of your dealings, and in return we will help you fight the pigs."

Everyone goes silent for a moment,

"OINK OINK!" Helmut shouts, breaking the tension and taking everybody by surprise.

The Don lets out a feeble laugh. "That is the deal."

"Great! Then we'll be in touch."

"Ehh, wait." Don Fontana stops him before he can leave. "I would like you to stay and enjoy a meal from our restaurant. After all, we are business partners now."

Helmut licks his lips. "I am pretty hungry... Why not!" He laughs, remaining in his seat.

"Zeta!" The Don calls for her and she rushes out of the kitchen. "Rustle up some lasagne for Don Baulsack and the rest of us, will you?"

"Yes, sir," she says and runs back into the kitchen.

Helmut turns back to The Don. "No schnitzel?" He smirks.

"We don't usually cater for Germans," Mario quips, passive-aggressively.

"But we can arrange something for the future," The Don adds, raising an eyebrow at

Mario.

Zeta returns with two plates; she scrutinises them before she puts them on the table.

"She's being way too obvious about it," Al panics.

Helmut observes the plate, and the people around the table,

"*Das ist eine Falle*," (It's a trap), he whispers to his guard, who now becomes much stiffer.

Al and Sonny hear this through the microphone and look at each other in fear.

"Shit, he knows." Al throws her head into her hands.

"What do we do?" Sonny panics.

"I don't know..."

As Zeta returns with two more plates, and all eyes are on her, Helmut switches his poisoned plate with Bella's without anyone noticing, apart from Aart Van de Jaager.

Everybody has a plate in front of them now, and they hold up a glass of wine to toast this new business venture.

"To life and new prospects," The Don says, and they all clink their glasses together.

Aart swallows hard as he sees Bella shovel in the first forkful of lasagne.

"Erm... Bella, I have something for you, from my son," he says, before she chews it too much.

"Which son?"

"Casper," he says quickly.

She rolls her eyes. "I don't want it."

Sweat begins to drip down his forehead onto his plate. Helmut finishes his meal in record time. He pats his belly and smiles.

"Delicious. What do you think, Bella?" He smirks at her.

"I think it's..." She stops, wide-eyed.

"What?" Luca asks, leaning closer to her.

She holds onto her neck and gasps for breath.

"Poisonous?" Helmut provides the word she is looking for.

Suddenly, a heavy foot beats open the staff door and Al and Sonny appear, brandishing pistols in each hand. They open fire and Helmut ducks for cover, but his guards are shot down instantly. The Fontanas rush to Bella's side and Luca injects her with the antidote.

Helmut, who is now crawling towards the entrance, making sure to use the furniture as a shield, whips out his own pistol and begins shooting back at the girls.

"He's going out the front!" Zeta shouts down the phone to Matteo from the safety of the kitchen.

Salva aims at the back door of Helmut's car parked at the front of the building, waiting for the perfect shot. Helmut clings onto the car door, shielding his head with his arm as bullets fly through the window, narrowly missing him, but puncturing the car.

"Now, Salva!" Matteo orders.

"Not yet," he says steadily.

"Salva, you'll miss your chance, do it now!"

"Not yet," he repeats, lining the red dot on Helmut's temple.

In the blink of an eye, as the bullets cease for a second, Helmut swings open the car door and the driver speeds off before he is even fully in the vehicle. Salva missed his chance.

"What the fuck are you doing?" Matteo cracks in anger. "*Stupido bastardo!*"

Salva cannot even bring himself to breathe, let alone stick up for himself. He knows he made a big mistake. He continues to stare blankly through the scope, wishing that Helmut would gracefully present himself in front of his sight again.

"Shit, he got away," Sonny says frustratedly, the pistols dropping to her side.

"Bella are you okay?" The Don asks his daughter.

She nods, and takes a sip of water.

"Zeta, how did you not get the plates right?" Luca snarls.

"I did! He must have swapped them!" She pleads for them to believe her.

Luca lets out a harsh laugh. "Oh yeah, like we could have missed him do that! Is losing one sibling not good enough for you?"

Zeta begins to cry into her hands.

Al walks over to her and puts her hand on her

shoulder. "Actually, Luca, I think he did swap them, check the CCTV," she tells him.

Luca's face softens and he wanders over to give Zeta a hug and to apologise for losing his temper with her.

"More importantly," Sonny begins, "Aart... What are you doing?" she questions him.

"This was part of my plan! I wasn't really going into business with him," he explains.

The Don stands up from Bella's side. "What about the Baulsacks you were supposed to be getting rid of?"

"They're already gone! I left it with Casper and Jelle."

"Don't you think you would have been more useful in Amsterdam rather than leaving your incapable son in charge?" The Don shouts.

"I thought I was doing the right thing." Aart takes the heat for Casper, it was his idea.

"Well, you thought wrong. Look at this mess, and we haven't even killed Helmut! There's gonna be an absolute shit storm coming now." Mario joins in on the argument now.

Aart sighs. "I understand now that what I did was wrong. I will make it up to you. Me and my sons will go to Berlin and kill him with our bare hands!"

"You've done enough, Aart," The Don starts. "The girls will be going." He looks at Al and Sonny. "Tomorrow."

Dear reader,

We hope you enjoyed reading *The Dons of Warington*. Please take a moment to leave a review, even if it's a short one. Your opinion is important to us.

Discover more books by Isobel Wycherley at https://www.nextchapter.pub/authors/isobel-wycherley

Want to know when one of our books is free or discounted? Join the newsletter at http://eepurl.com/bqqB3H

Best regards,

Isobel Wycherley and the Next Chapter Team

ABOUT THE AUTHOR

I was born on the 13th of September, 1999 in Warrington, England.

I wrote my first book when I was eighteen, based around my experiences in the summer of 2018.

I study linguistics at Manchester Metropolitan University, I am interested in pursuing forensic linguistics and have an interest in acquisition.

I love music, it's always been a big part of my life, as well as helping me to establish a positive attitude towards anything. Films are another love of mine, which I try to reflect in my writing style, since I generally picture my stories as films playing out in my head, which helps me to imagine what I would want to see happen next, if it really were a film.

I'm very inquisitive and want to know everything about everything. I love learning and experiencing new things and I can't wait to see where that takes me, especially in my new writing career.

Printed in Great Britain
by Amazon